FIRE SERMON

Also by Jamie Quatro

I Want to Show You More

FIRE SERMON

A NOVEL

JAMIE QUATRO

Grove Press
New York

Portions of this novel have appeared previously, in different form, in the *Oxford American*, *Ecotone*, *Forty Stories: New Writing from Harper Perennial*, and *The Sewanee Review*. Poetry in Section Two first appeared in *Blackbird* ("The Withholding"), *Oxford American* ("Protestant Worshipper"), the *Mississippi Review* ("Foreknowledge"), and in *BOMB*'s Word Choice poetry series ("Prayer").

Passages from *Bluets* used with permission by Maggie Nelson. Excerpts from "The Spirit and the Soul" from *Collected Poems* by Jack Gilbert, copyright © 2012 by Jack Gilbert. Used by permission of Alfred A. Knopf, an imprint of the Knopf Doubleday Publishing Group, a division of Penguin Random House LLC. All rights reserved; Excerpts from "The Talkers" from *Blood, Tin, Straw: Poems* by Sharon Olds, copyright © 1999 by Sharon Olds. Used by permission of Alfred A. Knopf, an imprint of the Knopf Doubleday Publishing Group, a division of Penguin Random House LLC. All rights reserved; Linda Gregg, excerpts f rom "Ravenous" and "Asking for Directions" from *Chosen by the Lion*. Copyright © 1994 by Linda Gregg. Reprinted with the permission of The Permissions Company, Inc. on behalf of Graywolf Press, Minneapolis, Minnesota, graywolfpress.org. Excerpt from "The Waste Land" from Collected Poems 1909-1962 by T. S. Eliot. Copyright 1936 by Houghton Mifflin Harcourt Publishing Company. Copyright © renewed 1964 by Thomas Steams Eliot. Reprinted by permission of Houghton Mifflin Harcourt Publishing Company. All rights reserved. Excerpt from *Selected Essays* by T. S. Eliot. Copyright 1950 by Houghton Mifflin Harcourt Publishing Company. Copyright © renewed 1978 by Esme Valerie Eliot. Reprinted by permission of Houghton Mifflin Harcourt Publishing Company. All rights reserved.

This book is a work of fiction. Any resemblance between these fictional characters and actual persons, living or dead, is purely coincidental.

First Grove Atlantic hardcover edition: January 2018

Printed in the United States of America

FIRST EDITION

ISBN 978-0-8021-2704-4
eISBN 978-0-8021-6555-8

Library of Congress Cataloging-in-Publication Data is available for this title.

Grove Press
an imprint of Grove Atlantic
154 West 14th Street
New York, NY 10011
Distributed by Publishers Group West
groveatlantic.com

18 19 20 21   10 9 8 7 6 5 4 3 2 1

In loving memory of my grandmother,
Naomi V. Utz

FIRE SERMON

Bhikkhus, all is burning.
And what is the all that is burning?

-*Buddha*,
The Fire Sermon

To Carthage then I came

Burning burning burning burning
O Lord Thou pluckest me out
O Lord Thou pluckest

burning

-*T. S. Eliot*,
The Waste Land

ONE

Shall we walk back? James asked outside the theater.

Chicago, April 2017. The air chilly, the sky cleared off after an evening of rain. We'd left the film a half hour after it began, a poorly written, poorly acted farce. Now the sidewalk was empty. Tiny lights strung between gas lamps and storefronts created a glittery canopy above us. *Charming,* he'd said when we arrived earlier, a part of the city neither of us had seen. I was still in my clothes from that morning: white sweater, pencil skirt, suede ankle boots with zippers, high-heeled.

I'll call a car, I said. Your hotel's on the way to mine.

We rode in silence, the wet asphalt glowing red and green at stoplights. When we pulled up to his hotel, James turned to face me, adjusting his glasses. Okay, he said. Text me when you're safely back. He leaned over to brush my cheek with his lips, but when the bellhop opened the rear door he didn't get out. He sat looking ahead, rubbing a hand up and down, up and down his thigh.

Both of us forty-five, born in the same year, four months apart; both married to our spouses for twenty-three years. Two similarities in what had come to seem, in the three years we'd known one another, a cosmically ordained accumulation: born and raised in the desert Southwest, allergic to peanuts, students of the Christian mystics and quantum theory and *Moby Dick*. Children the same ages and genders—older girl, younger boy—and ninety-six-year-old grandmothers who still lived independently. In the end it was this last fact that undid me, the longevity in our respective genes.

The safe way to let yourself fall in love with someone who isn't your spouse: imagine the life you might have together after both your spouses have passed away.

(What I mean is, darling: when I made love with you that night, I was making love with the magnificent old man I knew you would become.)

Can I help with any bags? the bellhop finally said.

You're at the Hyatt? James said to me.

Yes.

Take us to the Hyatt, he said to the driver, and pulled the door shut.

But this story begins where others end: a boy and a girl in love, a wedding, a happily-ever-after.

Malibu, June. A bride and four attendants on a grassy bluff above the Pacific. The morning is overcast, typical along the coast, the diffuse light ideal for photographs. The bride's dress is raw silk in antique ivory and appears backlit against the slate of ocean. Sweetheart neckline, cap sleeves, full skirt with a train that will later gather into a bustle. She cradles her bouquet like an infant, six dozen roses in various stages of bloom, blush pink. The groomsmen, fraternity brothers, have already been photographed. They wait inside the chapel, where in half an hour the ceremony will begin. They wear gray tuxedos with ascot ties and slick black shoes. Three, including the groom, have the same round tortoise-shell glasses.

Down the coast, at the country club in Pacific Palisades, the caterers are assembling the cake: five tiers frosted in a basket-weave pattern, with real ivy and roses trailing down one side. The bride has selected a different flavor for each tier: butter cream, chocolate, spice, red velvet. The top layer—which will be placed in the couple's freezer for their first anniversary, until one night while they're out, the bride's younger brother, stoned and knowing nothing about such traditions, eats the whole thing—is white chocolate with raspberry-creme filling. The centerpieces are fishbowls with ivy and roses identical to those on the cake. They sit in a refrigerated van on Pacific Coast Highway, north of Sunset. The driver is stuck in beach traffic.

But there is plenty of time.

The bride's brother, age fifteen, is tasked with decorating the limo. *Just married,* he writes over and over in soap paint. How many times is too many? He draws a wedding bell but it comes out looking like a top hat so he wipes it away. He reaches into his pocket to feel the rings. Today is the first time he's heard himself introduced to other people as a man. *Margaret's little brother, the Best Man.*

The bride's sister is a senior in high school and bewildered by her role. The other bridesmaids seem to know what to talk about, how to look and act. She wonders why her sister didn't ask one of them to be the maid of honor. She hardly knows her sister now. When she'd left home she wore frosty pink lipstick and bleached her naturally auburn hair; now she wears no makeup and has let her hair go dark. She talks of fellowships and stipends and moving to Princeton, where in the fall she'll start graduate school. Her fiancé—husband— will work in Manhattan.

You'll have to come visit us, her sister said. It's student housing, converted army barracks, nothing fancy. But we'll have a spare room.

The bride's mother is forty-four, her father forty-six; both look young enough to be the ones getting married. Delight, pride, tears. Their oldest daughter, graduated summa cum laude in three years, marrying the first boy she ever seriously dated. So mature for her age, so self-possessed! And now this presidential fellowship. She'll be one of the youngest PhDs in the country when she's finished. An expert in something called postcolonial theory.

And what will her husband do? guests ask.

A job in *New York City,* her parents tell them. Consulting firm, financial services.

Inside the chapel the wedding guests gather. Shuffle of programs, subdued talk, the organ playing Handel and Mozart, sotto voce. The ushers—also fraternity brothers— lead the three widowed grandmothers (two on the bride's side, one on the groom's), and then the mothers, down the aisle. The groom's mother uses a cane, the stepfather walking just behind. The groom's parents divorced when he was three, and his father was not invited to the wedding. The groom is an only child. An orphan, for all intents and purposes, he's told the bride over the years.

Today he will get a new family: lawyer father-in-law, middle school principal mother-in-law. Two siblings, two hale grandmothers.

He's a good listener, the bride told her parents. You should see him with children. You should hear him play the guitar.

I realize you're getting the raw end of this deal, he'd said to the bride, the day of their engagement.

I'm getting you, she said.

The groom is agnostic but it doesn't bother her, when it comes to his actions he's a better Christian than most Christians she knows; in fact he is—she can think of no better word—*malleable.* Alters his demeanor to meet the needs of others. His voice acquires a tenderness when he speaks to his mother on the phone, as if he's tucking her in. His thick hair, the way his lips part and his tongue presses against his bottom teeth before he speaks—a deep thoughtfulness about him.

Thomas knows how to handle Margaret, her mother has said to close friends, a few relatives. He respects our beliefs. And he knows how to put up with . . . well, a certain volatility in her temperament. She'll go hard after something and once she gets it no longer care. A hammered gold necklace she pestered me to buy for a year . . . she wore it twice and gave it away.

The groomsmen are lined up, the minister front and center. The bridesmaids come in too fast, but the flower girl—three-year-old daughter of the bride's cousin—takes her time. From her basket she removes petals singly, squats to place each onto the fabric runner as if affixing stickers. No one hurries her, she is precious, cameras flash. Finally the pause, hush. The silence grows uncomfortable until the groom's mother grabs her cane and pushes herself up. The organ notes blast and, with a great creaking and rustling, the guests rise and turn. Only then does the bride's mother realize she forgot to stand first, the one thing required of her this day.

When the bride appears the groom staggers. He reaches a hand to steady himself against the best man, who doesn't notice. (He's thinking about the rings: Does the bride give the groom the ring first? Or is it the reverse?) The father smiles to the audience, looking right, left, white teeth flashing against his smooth, darkly tanned skin, the bride's face misty in an iridescent veil. Who gives this woman? In his practiced courtroom voice, the father makes a practiced speech: *This is a moment of great honor and pride in the life of any father, but it is a particular moment of honor and pride for me, and for her mother, to give our firstborn daughter in marriage today, in the sight of the Lord and these many witnesses.* He lifts the veil and kisses a bright cheek. The bride turns and hands the bouquet to her sister, who until this moment didn't know that holding the flowers for the duration of the ceremony would be her responsibility. She doesn't know what to do with her own bouquet. She mashes the two together and clutches them against her chest.

A short homily, traditional vows, the exchange of rings (brother produces from pocket, feels immediately hungry, starving in fact, wonders if there will be actual meat or just chicken at the reception), lighting of the Unity Candle, two flames becoming one. Leave and cleave. The groom surprises the bride and sings to her, a groomsman handing him a uku-lele. Laughter, tears, the kiss—a short one—and the organ charges out the recessional triplets. The couple exits, arm in arm, waving to guests.

But the bride has forgotten her bouquet. The sister must walk down the aisle with it. Outside the chapel she discovers the bride and groom have been whisked off for photos. She puts the bouquet beneath a stone bench to keep it safe, but in the flurry of hugs and kisses and photographs, the confused clambering into limousines, the flowers are left behind. An hour into the reception the bride realizes her mistake. She asks a friend to go back and look, but by the time the friend gets to the chapel, the bouquet is gone.

Tucked into the de-thorned roses was a linen handker-chief from the bride's paternal grandmother, the color of a robin's egg—something old, borrowed, and blue—hand-embroidered in white: *DTH*.

Whose initials, Gran? she'd asked.

Oh, just someone I used to know, her grandmother said.

Twenty-five years later, when the grandmother dies of congestive heart failure (three months on an oxygen tank, *How it hurts* her last words) the forty-six-year-old granddaughter will receive a padded envelope in the mail. Inside will be eleven handkerchiefs, each identical to the one she lost on her wedding day, and a letter in her grandmother's wavering cursive.

June 13, 1993

My darling Mags,

I've just returned from your wedding. What a lovely
ceremony! And I adore Thomas. We all do. He'll be
a wonderful husband. Your mother says you lost the
hankie. No matter. As you see, I have more. His name
was Donald Trent Harper. I met him the summer I
stayed at Ruth's lake house. Do you remember Auntie
Ruth, from Michigan? The one who always wore
jeweled cords on her spectacles? Don was a horseman.
He was twenty-seven, ten years older than I was. That
summer we fell in love and decided to get married.
When I got back to Cleveland we had an argument over
the telephone. Something silly, I don't remember what.
But I was rude. I insulted him and hung up. I was too
proud to be the one to call back and apologize; I wanted
him to call first. I waited a year but he never called.
I married your grandpa Jack to spite Don, and when

Jack died so young, I didn't remarry—not because, as
I always told your father, I could never love anyone as
much as I loved Jack, but because I hoped Donald and I
might someday find one another again. Which of course
we never did.

Well, my darling, now you know. I embroidered
one hankie a month the year I waited for the telephone
to ring. I should like it very much if you kept them.
Perhaps they'll remind you to always be the one to call
back first.

Loving you,
Gran

P.S. I trust you won't share this with your father.
There's no harm in his believing I only ever loved your
grandfather. I did love him, in my own way.

Cosmically ordained. Foolish, the way lovers scaffold passion with symbology, constructing a joint past which seems, even after a few hours, immemorial. Let us sing the litany of events that transpired before the moment we met. Love's Old Testament. They recur to it often—remember this, remember that. Israelites in the desert, telling one another the old, old stories.

How foolish we were, I tell myself now, hoping someday the word will sound true.

James saw me first, the first time we met in person. July 2014, the conference in Nashville. We'd been writing to one another for almost a year. I was wearing a scoop-neck blouse, long skirt, flip-flops. My hair pulled back, no makeup. In the reception room a table was laid out with fruit and pastries, coffee and sweet tea. From across the room I heard him say my name. *Maggie.* There you are, I thought. Here you are, in my home state. He was wearing a navy button-down, khaki shorts, loafers with no socks. My traveling shoes, he said later, when he took them off.

I tripped over the table leg to get to him. He stood waiting, one hand on his hip, the other holding a folder with his agenda inside. I felt he wanted to watch me approach, to study the way I moved; I imagined he felt that any movement on his end would dull his pleasure in watching. The look on his face was one I would become familiar with, whenever we were together: amusement on the surface, admiration beneath. A kind of ease, something already understood. *We belong to one another.*

I shook his hand. Tattooed on his wrist: the word *sight*. Later, at lunch, I'd notice the other wrist: *vision*.

I've been looking for you everywhere, he said. His bottom teeth were crooked, pleasingly so.

I've been around, I said. It's nice to meet you in person, finally.

Likewise. Though a bit surreal. Are you coming to my talk?

Of course. I wouldn't miss it.

And after?

I'm free all afternoon, I said. What's on your agenda?

You're my agenda, he said.

The bride's parents hired a professional videographer to film the ceremony. Two camera angles inside the chapel, to capture both the bride's and groom's faces. If you, an outsider, were to watch the video, you would see a young man with dark hair and broad chest, twenty-four, a bit green in the face, nearly crippled with gratitude and longing; you would see a girl, just twenty-one, with long auburn hair, eager to play her part. You would see the way they looked at one another, as the camera switched angles: bride blinking back tears and glancing from groom's face to audience; groom bowing his head and nodding during the homily.

You would see what everyone there saw: a boy and a girl in love.

What you wouldn't see is a day three years earlier, in the backseat of Thomas's car, when Maggie was a freshman. His hand pushing hard on the back of her neck to force her mouth farther down, so deep her throat constricts and her eyes water, and how she tries to stifle the sound of her gagging, she doesn't want him to feel bad for how he's hurting her, he can't know that what he's doing hurts, he's simply carried away by his need—abandoned, as he was, by his mother. He can't help it, she tells herself.

Nor would you have seen them, two nights before the car, alone in his dorm room when he told her about his childhood in Philadelphia, his father's drug addiction and how his mother left town for good when he was ten, and how when he realized the deep trouble his father was in he went to Pittsburgh to ask if he could live with her. *My dad used to ask me for money, I mean I was in sixth grade and he'd ask if I could get money off my friends. I took his cash and credit card and got myself onto a bus. My mom sent me back. She knew what my dad was into and she sent me back,* he told her—his hand up her shirt, then inside her pants. She let him do what he wanted, this was a way she could comfort him, and anyhow her own body was responding to the kinds of touches she wouldn't allow in high school—and now she's on her back on his mattress, he's taken off her shirt and pants and, with a finger, hooked the edge of her panties up, inserted himself beneath, *Don't worry, I'll just rub on the outside, I can make you come that way and then I'll finish myself* but against her will she is grabbing him, she is pulling him hard against her. *Are you sure?* he says. *Please,* she says, almost crying, *please,* hears herself saying the word though she knows it isn't the word she should say, not the word her best self would say—she doesn't know Thomas, if he's the right one for this moment—but right now, best self be damned. He pushes, hard. Twice, three times. Some pain beneath the pleasure, but the pleasure outweighs, she comes on the third push, comes again before he slides out and falls onto her belly.

A wet heat between his navel and hers. He hands her some tissues. She wipes her stomach and presses a clean tissue up between her thighs, trying not to wince.

I'm sorry, Thomas says. I pushed you too far.

No, she says. I wanted you to.

Back in her own dorm, her roommate asleep, she goes into the bathroom and washes herself with soap and water. She changes into her pajamas, kneels on the rough blue carpet beside her bed, and confesses to the God who has already seen what she's done (and can you, reading this, forgive the self-indulgent, almost laughable repentance, berating herself for what is only normal, and expected? But recall: she is barely eighteen, her first kiss was only a year ago) that she has sinned. Fornicated. Had sex before marriage. Something she's sworn she would never do.

Ridiculous, she will think, years into her marriage. Ludicrous, the standard I set for myself.

Beside her dormitory bed, with the sharp tip of a piece of sea glass she'd found on the beach that morning, she cuts a tiny groove in her forearm, tastes her blood in the dark, and tells God—only thinking the words in her head—that she will marry Thomas. Promises to go through with it, no matter what.

I have made my bed and now will lie in it, she prays. This man will be my husband. I will honor your will in this way.

Only let him be a good husband, she prays.

You're my agenda—the day the light changed, the air turned liquid. After lunch we took a long walk around the Vanderbilt campus, where James was staying. He was teaching a community workshop the following day. Dorm, chapel, dining hall, Bicentennial Oak—each placed in its precise location for us, for the moment we would arrive, and notice. A universe of forms bending its knee. Somewhere a bell chimed the hour. It was hot out. James kept wiping his neck with a handkerchief, refolding it into a neat triangle, and tucking it into his breast pocket.

He: I was twelve when I developed the allergy, home alone and my throat started to swell shut. The hospital was eight blocks away. Thank God my father had taught me to drive. Those minutes in the car were such a rush. The thrill of driving in traffic, the reduced oxygen—knowing there were two ways I could die before I got to the hospital. I've gone looking for that feeling ever since.

She: My first dissertation was going to be on postcolonial reinterpretations of the Genesis story, but I'd started writing on the sly—stories, poetry—and I just couldn't keep going. Theory felt thinner and thinner the deeper I got into it. And then as you know we got pregnant with Kate. She saved me from the comp lit path. Later I got interested in the Hellenistic view of history versus the Christian, cyclical versus linear, and Old Testament versus New Testament eschatological outlooks. Things spiraled from there.

He: I read them everything when they were little. Dickens, Milton, Shakespeare. Moby Dick in its entirety. Caroline must have been eight but she listened to every word.

She: I read it to Tommy when he was nine. Moby Dick's *wasted on the young. Not the language, of course. But Ahab, the horror and disgust you feel—you have to reach midlife to realize Melville's pointing the finger.*

He: Ah, but at what? We all have a white whale to chase? Or the chase itself will turn us into monsters unless we give it up?

She: Both, I guess.

The party on campus that night: James on the front porch talking with a faculty member. I was sitting on the steps. When I picked up my backpack and stood to leave, I saw him step back and shake hands with the professor. The assumption: We would leave together. We would do everything together, whenever we were together.

I knew we'd get along, he said, as soon as we were alone. I knew it when I read your letters. I've saved them all. And your book. Astonishing. You said you write poetry?

A little, yeah. Secretly.

We walked toward the house he was staying in, the opposite direction from my car. Halfway there I stopped.

I should get home, I said. Do you want to meet for breakfast?

Of course, he said. (And he was there in front of the dining hall, watching me approach—on his face that mix of amusement/admiration/pleasure.) I reached up to give him a hug but because of my backpack he couldn't return the embrace. He squeezed my shoulders instead.

So you'll send me a poem, he said.

I'd be too embarrassed.

One poem. I want you to promise.

I don't have anything ready.

I'm not letting you go till you say it: James, I promise to send you a poem.

I promise to send you a poem.

Good. See you tomorrow.

Each step a soft sinking into earth, walking back to my car, battling the urge to turn around. *Fight like heaven,* a minister once said in a sermon on temptation. *Engage in the battle like you mean it.* I'd battled before but it was nothing like this, nothing like the battle it would become nearly three years later, after the aborted film in Chicago, *Take us to the Hyatt*—his hand now on the seat between us, tips of his fingers touching my thigh.

Thomas is, in fact, a good husband. He works long hours so she can stay in grad school full-time. Sometimes she takes the train in and they spend weekends in the city. They stay in the Mansfield in midtown, or when they're in the Village, the Washington Square Hotel, where Bob Dylan lived with Joan Baez. A friend gives them tickets to see Ralph Fiennes and Tara Fitzgerald in *Hamlet*, sixth-row orchestra seats.

He cooks for her, breakfasts, dinners. He doesn't like cats but when she brings home a long-haired kitten, black and gray, he strokes it and says he doesn't mind the litter pan in the shower stall. He goes to church with her, even prays with her if she asks him too. Reads drafts of her essays, does her laundry when she's writing papers. Holds back her hair when she begins to vomit every morning, supports her decision to quit the doctoral program and cries when, after eighteen hours of labor and a vacuum extraction, their daughter comes into the world. No epidural, an episiotomy to make space for the vacuum head, a pain beyond pain that causes her to leave her body, not floating outside of it but descending so deeply inside it's as if she's no longer attached. *I know it hurts like hell, hurts like hell, hurts like hell*—the doctor's voice repeating the words she cannot speak for herself while the baby is pulled out and she is pulled away from the doctor and nurses, away from Thomas, descending through interior darkness toward a tiny closet with the dimensions of a single cell. Into this space I must burrow, she thinks, or I will die.

The suction leaves a round bulb atop the baby's skull. Our two-headed darling, Thomas says, watching the nurse show him how to swaddle.

Two years later she has an emergency C-section with their son. Thomas isn't allowed into the operating room until they've done the spinal block. An intern misplaces the needle. I need my husband, Maggie says, before losing consciousness. When she wakes the intern's eyes are inches from hers. Your blood pressure dropped, the intern says, but you're okay now. A screen is drawn up between her head and lower body. Thomas comes in, scrubbed and wearing blue from head to foot, his eyes the only thing she can see. She doesn't know the mechanics of the procedure; she feels pressure and tugging and imagines her father at the lake, reaching beneath the dark surface of the water to net a hooked fish.

The baby emerges rump-first, the cord twisted four times around his neck. So much blood on the body, so unlike her daughter's appearance, the birth canal and draining amniotic fluid a natural first bath. This baby is white with protective wax like the hard exteriors on cheeses she cuts away to access the soft inner parts. A nurse lifts him over the screen and she kisses a bloody ear, the part of him closest to her mouth. For the rest of her life, it's what she will remember, remembering his birth—that tiny, reticulate, red-and-white ear.

While they sew her up, Thomas tells her she's incredible. Heroic. The bravest woman in the world.

She is allowed no food—so much gas trapped inside, from the exposure to air, she can feel it in her shoulders and neck. She must expel before they'll let her eat anything, or allow her to go home. Forty-eight hours pass. Stool softeners, laxatives, suppositories, nothing. Unbearable. Her breasts swollen and leaking, colostrum giving way to the pressure of first milk. Stitches, staples, swollen ankles, dry lips. The third day she takes off the hospital gown and puts on leggings and a tunic. I can't stand this any longer, she says to Thomas, I feel like an animal. A nurse administers an enema and she cries, more from the humiliation and the anticipation of relief than the pain, and when it happens there is no warning. The outfit is ruined. She changes back into a gown and walks to the nursery to feed the baby.

When she returns she hears water running in the bathroom and opens the door to see Thomas kneeling beside the tub, lifting the leggings to his nose. His neck turns splotchy when he sees her. I wanted to make sure I got them clean, he says, I didn't want you to have to think about it when we got home. A moment she'll come back to, over the years, the intense shame she felt—not that she'd soiled her clothing, but that her husband could, and did, love her in such a way. Embracing what was filthy in her.

Nineteen years later, at the Hyatt in Chicago—just after she and James have climaxed together for the first time—she will think of the hospital and will feel, at first, only gratitude for the fact she no longer inhabits that animal-body. That she has emerged from the child-rearing years with a still-desirable form. She'll go into the bathroom, lock the door, kneel in front of the toilet and vomit. *Thomas cleaning backed-up shit out of her pants. Thomas rinsing the tub so the nurses wouldn't have to do it.* She'll brush her teeth and wash her face and walk back into the room. Fuck me again, she'll say to James, the only way to drive the image from her mind. And he will, he will fuck her again. He will pin her arms and, with his tongue, make a line from her neck downward, pausing to penetrate the deep well of her navel and trace the thin white scar above the rubbled hair.

*S*o you've come to me, again, because you keep falling in love with men who aren't your husband. Is that correct?

I don't keep falling. James was the first.

Let me remind you that the last time you came, it was because of the Aquinas professor. You said you thought you were falling in love.

I was wrong last time.

Let me remind you that before the professor, there was the minister; before the minister, your husband's MBA friend. You claimed to be in love with each.

Wrong each time.

How do you know you're not wrong this time?

The others were preparation. The exposure of inferiors before the revelation of the ideal. Didn't God first parade the animals in front of Adam and ask him to find a suitable partner among them?

And now that you have found Eve, you believe you will stop looking?

Yes.

What if it's the acquisition you're in love with, not the person? What if your so-called love for James, once exhausted, begins to dissipate, then transfers itself to the next in line?

There won't be a next in line.

You said that with the Aquinas professor.

The professor was a prop jet. James is a fucking 747.

Either way, if you want to stay married, you might not want to leave the ground.

I know.

I know I know I know I know I know.

May 2017

Dear God:

Can you forgive someone for an act they cannot repent of?
I knew in the elevator—knew in the car—what was about
to happen. Did nothing to stop it. It's been a month now
and asking your forgiveness would mean seeing that night
as sinful, but to preserve the memory I cannot let myself see
it that way. Yet this is what you demand of me. To call the
memories *scales*, let them fall from my eyes so I will see the
evil behind the pleasure—*using* the pleasure to draw me away
from you. Away from Thomas, the children. But I've lost him,
he's out there leading his magnificent life and I'm still here in
the silence of not telling, so can you at least allow me the
memory, unrepented? Let me keep it, God. Let me have the
woman on the elevator, the man beside her, let me keep what
the two of them did in room 1602, let it always be happening
(and shall I pray, Let Christ always be dying for the pain that
moment caused, and is still causing? What about the pleasure? Did he die to remove that too? How am I supposed to
ask forgiveness for feeling what my body only naturally—)

Dear James:

I keep trying to write my prayers out longhand, in a journal,
and end up wishing I was writing to you instead. So be it. I'm
reading a book about the color blue. Brief poetic numbered

passages. I read a few each morning and think about them all day and it's like holding bits of candy in my mouth. The author writes about renunciation, says that when you give something up—alcohol, drug, person—it leaves a void inside of you that something else will rush in to fill. Augustine's God-shaped hole. But some people, she says, realize the emptiness itself is God. That a Zen master once described enlightenment as *Lots of space and nothing holy*.

I have this space in me and God is not there and emptiness is not there. What is there is this conversation we can no longer have, since our agreement in Chicago.

I read an interview with a poet yesterday, someone you mentioned knowing. He said that when he was a boy he climbed the tree beside his house to gather apples. Sitting in the top branches, looking through an upstairs window, he saw the inside of his bedroom—from that vantage it looked like a room he'd never seen—and instantly his desire for apples fell away. He forgot about them completely. And there's that Jack Gilbert poem (I know you don't trust him as a poet but I can't help loving him) about going into an apple orchard to gather fruit but coming out with scent and dappled light and a wide sense of the passage of time.

Both poets insist, in hindsight, they weren't after apples— the apples were only a lure toward something else. The first poet said that just as he went after apples when he was young, so he went after the bodies of women when he was older. But his desire for women, too, dropped away, and what was left—the thing he realized he'd been after all along—was God. God was luring him through apples, through women, through sex. Once he realized it was God, the poet said, he began to understand that God, too, was a lure.

But he never said what the thing beyond God was—what God was luring him *toward*. I suspect it's a boomerang: sex a lure to God, God a lure back to sex, ad infinitum.

How I want to rip these pages out and send them to you. Or call you on the phone and talk, the way we used to.

Their second year in Princeton, Thomas and Maggie move out of married student housing to take a job as houseparents at a boarding school for a famous boy choir. Nights and weekend duties only, free room and board in return. She drives Thomas to the Dinky each morning so he can get to Princeton Junction, and from there to Penn Station. She attends her doctoral seminars in the mornings, teaches English at the boys' school in the afternoons.

Their apartment is in the main mansion, the former servants' quarters. A row of windows in their bedroom looks onto the back porch, now enclosed as a locker room, the place the boys dump their backpacks. On weekends they can't sleep in, the boys are there at first light, Good morning, Miss, Good morning, Sir, can we play basketball, can we walk into town, can I get into my candy closet. Every day, all day, the singing—tour choir, choir A, choir B, resident training choir. When she returns from campus, or after a run, walking the last bit up the driveway toward the mansion—brick, symmetrical, dormered and pillared—the high clear notes carry out through the open windows and catch in the branches of the trees surrounding the property, eighteen acres of grounds designed by Frederick Law Olmsted, the famous landscape architect.

The boys leave anonymous notes in her mailbox, tokens of puppy love. *I heart you, miss. You're my favorite teacher. I like your hair.* She is twenty-three, twenty-four, around her they can begin to imagine the men they will become. The bolder ones wait, in the mornings, just outside the door that opens onto the mansion's main hallway. You smell good today, miss, they say when she emerges. You smell like fruit.

What is it, the invisible thing that makes boys and men want to be close to her? What Thomas calls, awkwardly, her uncorked-ness? You're like a just-opened bottle of fine wine, Thomas says. She possesses, a friend tells her, an exterior softness: there is no protective shell, she trusts everyone, finds everyone interesting, is honest to a fault. Raised in love, money, and the certainty of God's favor—money the *indication* of God's favor, an idea so insidious she won't recognize it till she's in her forties. She has never been broken up with, or betrayed, has never seen anyone die. All the eagerness and desire of her youth were fixed in time by the marriage; the wedding sealed off the potential for the kinds of letdowns others absorbed—failed relationships, cheating boyfriends. The fact of her early marriage ensured she would stay, for a space of many years, desirable. *A woman becomes more attractive as she ages only if she's married*, a male professor once told her. *It means you have something another man wanted, and still wants. It's single women who don't age well.*

The youngest boys come to visit in the evenings. They want to talk about their parents and siblings and friends at home. Sometimes they're so homesick they cry. She isn't supposed to touch them but she does, she's a believer in the Big Hug, can feel the tension leaving their limbs. Surrogate parent—shouldn't it be part of the job?

One evening before Christmas break, a sixth-grade boy named Nathan knocks on their door. He comes into the kitchen, shuffling his feet and looking all around, soft blond hair on his forehead like a swirl of cake frosting. He unlids the matryoshka dolls on her counter and sets them out—fat Santa within fat Santa—each one holding a different object. Bell, cake, miniature decorated tree. For a long time he doesn't speak.

How are exams going? she says to break the silence.

I need to tell you something, he says.

He sits on the rug in front of the kitchen cupboards, cross-legged, as if it's circle time in preschool. She does the same.

The older boys, he says. Sometimes they have these, like, contests?

He's looking at her, anguished, desperate for her to understand.

Contests, she says.

Like, to see how far they can—you know. Make it go.

In her mind she's searching. Spitting tobacco? Peeing off balconies?

Mostly they do it to themselves, Nathan says. But Hank does it to some of the younger boys. He, like, demonstrates.

His voice cracks, and something in the way he keeps flipping his hair and in the softness of his cheek skin, the delicate way he opens and closes his lips—she understands.

And Hank did this to you, she says.

I *asked him to*, Nathan says. The words come out like a growl. He begins to cry, great noisy sobs. She sits beside him and puts an arm around his shoulders. He leans in and lays his head against her chest.

When Thomas gets home he finds them there, sitting on the floor.

Hey, Thomas says. What's up?

Nathan stands. I want to go home, he says.

Thomas is the one who goes with Nathan to the head-master, Thomas the one who drives him to the airport in Newark and sits with him at the gate and tells him, over and over: It's okay, no one blames you, your parents will love you no matter what.

Years later their own sixth-grade son will kiss a girl in the preteen club on a cruise, and she'll remember Nathan, his soft wet eyelashes; how that evening, sitting on the floor in her kitchen, leaning against her, he put his hand beneath her breast, cupping, as if to test his own internal response system. How she allowed it for one second, and then gently, firmly pushed the hand away. He'd be in college now. Maybe the touch was a parting gesture to the hypothetical world of women; maybe it was simply a comfort. Either way, she doesn't regret allowing it.

May 2017

Dear James,

Another journal entry, another letter I'll never send. Like praying into the void. God of God, Light of Light, Very Void of Very Void—do you remember the day we went to the museum? The first day of the conference in Chicago, when we were still trying to pretend. There was a room in the contemporary wing with a film playing on loop, paper marionettes in silhouette. In the background, hanging from a tree, was a black man with a noose around his neck, his body swaying back and forth; in the foreground, the nude midsection of a white man with an erection. A succession of black females approached, knelt, and put their mouths on it. Over and over they moved their paper heads up and down until the white man shoved them away. None of them good enough. He ended up finishing himself while some kind of elated field music played, banjos and trumpets.

We sat on the bench and watched, the only two in the room. I was frozen between the horror of the imagery and the thrill of your body beside me in the dark. Watching that physical act on the screen made it impossible not to think of it with you. What would you have done, had I turned, as I wanted to, and kissed the smooth place on your neck just beneath your ear? Or placed my hand on your chest to feel the soft pectorals beneath your shirt, the contrast to Thomas's definition? (Another source of my arousal, the fusion of masculine and feminine in the shape of your body.) Did you sense what a thin membrane separated my thought from action? Perhaps you did, perhaps that's the reason you stood, abruptly, and left. In the gallery outside you were facing the mirrored wall, and when I came out, I saw you see me in reflection: the down, up brush of your eyes. As if you finally allowed yourself to look at more than just my face because in reflection I was at one remove from reality. Same purse of your lips and backward tilt of your head, that pleased expression I can't explain. Was it aesthetic pleasure only—something in my shape, or clothing, or the way I walked? Or was it—as I thought then, and still think now—ownership? *As much of you as my retina can hold, and electrify, and send along the optic nerve to my visual cortex—exactly this much of you belongs to me.*

The all-important gaze. I think it's the moment you knew I would bend. You sensed the perversely submissive thing inside me—I wanted pain from your hand, yours alone. Looking at me, in the mirror, you brought it into being. Wave function collapse: in taking my measurement all probabilities spiked to a single outcome. And you would do more than expose the desire, you would ravage it and walk away and I wouldn't try to stop you, or want you to stop. I also knew the crucial thing: *you wouldn't act.* You felt, and saw me feel back, saw that I was powerless, and decided to withhold. You, like Thomas, are a good man. A man who honors long-standing commitment. I saw you decide to go on being that man.

When I approached you took three steps away, in case I crossed a line. Which I would have, with the slightest nod of your head. I was a fucking wreck that day.

Later, in the park, we sat on another bench. So warm out, unseasonable, my feet were swelling in my heels. When I took them off I was startled for a moment by the color of my toenails, painted electric blue. I'd forgotten. We were talking about God and theology (the delight, the utter joy of speaking with someone who shared the language of my childhood). We discussed sullied words like *perfection,* how it has retained its original sense—a property of something that has been completed—only in music (perfect cadence) and grammar (perfect tense). We discussed the ontological versus cosmological arguments for the existence of God, and whether the universe exists *in esse,* like a house (deism, Aristotle) or *in fieri,* liquid in a vessel (theism, Aquinas). And St. John of the Cross, how he said we might become sexually aroused in the middle of spiritual acts, such as prayer, or communion, because when the spirit is moved to pleasure it drags the body up with it. We're holistic creatures, it cannot be helped.

What a *gracious* thing to have written, you said.

And you spoke of your father, who'd just passed away. He was a jazz musician, and the way he thrashed his limbs in the final hours looked as if he were trying but failing to suss out a drum rhythm.

He taught me to tie my own flies, you said, and I remember noticing how small his hands were. I inherited them. I've always been embarrassed by them.

You held a hand out to show me; I pressed my palm against it, the tips of my fingers an inch above yours.

An intimate conversation, comfortable. Familial, even, as if we were siblings. When I leaned over and put my head in your lap, did you know it wasn't a premeditated move? My body simply went there of its own volition. I wanted something. Not sexual.

Rest, maybe. I wanted to be at rest with you.

I closed my eyes and felt your hand on my forehead.

We cannot allow this, you said. We *will not* allow it.

Of course not, I said.

And yet: to sit up, I had to push, hard, against the downward force of your hand.

Shut it down, says Head.

Continue on, says Heart.

Deluded Heart, you'll only make a mess.

Deluded Head, any mess will be worth it.

You will watch fire consume everything you care about. You will be left with ash—the proper and only end of any burning.

Think of Moses. His vision in the desert. A bush on fire yet unconsumed.

Think of *Letters of John Newton:* the burning bush is an emblem applicable to the state of a Christian when she is in the fire of temptation. Think of Job, the true cause of his uncommon sufferings. Think how the experiment played upon him answered many good purposes: Job was humbled yet approved; his friends were instructed; the wisdom and mercy of the Lord, in his darkest dispensations, were gloriously—

Job is bullshit. Job lost everything.

Who are we to question God's ways, says Head. Who are you—

I want what I want, says Heart.

When Kate is two and Tommy a newborn, Maggie's rich uncle—her father's older brother, who never married—passes away, leaving his nieces and nephew a million dollars apiece. Thomas quits his job and they move to Nashville so he can start his MBA at the Owen School. They buy a house in Franklin, a subdivision eager to proclaim its connection to the pastoral: Maple Creek Farms. The houses are situated amid rolling hills and small lakes, a running and bike trail along a creek in the woods.

I think we should have them baptized, Maggie says one Sunday afternoon.

They've started attending a Presbyterian church, liberal, liturgical: robes, choir, stained glass. The kind of services Thomas doesn't mind. Short sermons, the subdued administration of the Lord's Supper once a month; infant baptisms, formal, with a tiny clear bowl into which the minister dips three fingers, then places them on the child's head. They'd seen a baptism that morning, a set of newborn twins.

Isn't Kate a little old? Thomas says.

My parents keep saying they want us to have them dedicated, next time we come home, she says. This is a way to avoid it.

Sure. I'm just surprised we haven't discussed it.

Her parents' church is an embarrassment to both of them: drums and electric guitars, flashing laser lights and images projected onto screens during the sermon, Madonna-and-child cloud formations in distant galaxies—the whole *performance*. And the constant talk of the second coming, the Israel-watching. *They need their own state, they need to rebuild the temple, America needs to help them keep what is rightfully theirs.* When she was growing up the threat of Jesus's return was fused with the threat of nuclear war; she used to dream of a mushroom cloud blooming over the mountains. Her own children, she thinks, will have God without dread.

She invites her parents to Nashville for the service, but they can't come, or won't; she can't tell. Tommy wears a gown and sleeps in Thomas's arms; Kate wears a new pink dress with a smocked chest. She keeps lifting and lowering the skirt, hiding her eyes, exposing to the congregation her new striped undies.

Father, name your child, the minister says.

Katherine Margaret Ellmann.

Katherine Margaret, I baptize you in the name of the Father, Son, and Holy Ghost. May the blessing of God Almighty be upon you.

Kate looks up at the minister, mouth open, blond curls on her forehead dark with water. The minister gathers Tommy into his arms. *Thomas Maxwell Ellmann Junior.* The minister repeats the blessing while the baby sleeps, pacifier quivering. And then the part of the ceremony Maggie loves: the minister carries Tommy up and down the aisles, she and Thomas following behind, Thomas carrying Kate, while the congregation sings the doxology. Maggie notices people wiping tears.

Afterward they stand in the foyer, as is the custom on baptismal Sundays, so the congregants can extend the right hand of fellowship. *So happy to have you here. Such beautiful children. What a lovely family.*

I see why you like it, Thomas says on the way home. Church. The sense of community. Who knows, maybe someday I'll join.

You know it doesn't matter to me, she says.

Yeah it does. It's a huge part of your life.

Well, it doesn't have to be part of yours.

Thomas reads to Kate before bed. Together they linger over pages. *Can you find the kitten? Can you find the clock? Where's Goldbug?* In the bedroom across the hall Maggie nurses the baby, listening for the soft *pock* of her daughter's thumb each time she pulls it from her mouth to point. She notices the way Thomas forms gentle edges around certain words: *chirp, basket, clatter.* A good father. She is lucky to be married to such a man.

When Kate is tucked in and she's finished nursing, Thomas takes the sleeping baby and places him, on his side, in a wedge-shaped prop in the bassinet. He remembers which direction the baby faced the previous night and alternates sides, to facilitate the development of an evenly shaped head—something she'd read in a parenting book and mentioned to him, once. Thomas remembers things like that. The way she likes her sheets tucked in tight, and how to separate the laundry, not just colors from whites but also linens from clothing, and how she likes her coffee, cream poured into the mug first and preheated, for twenty-three seconds, in the microwave.

After the children are asleep she brushes her teeth and leaves the water running, then sits on the closed toilet lid and breathes, trying to keep the boxed-in feeling from coming over her. It comes anyhow. She pictures scenes from sexy movies they've watched together: a heavy breast hanging above a waiting mouth, women tongue-kissing men, women tongue-kissing women. Nothing. She cannot manufacture arousal.

You love him, she tells herself. If he asks—when he asks—he's only asking you to love him like a normal wife.

But the panic overtakes her, the long pause between heartbeats, pressure in her chest before the rapid-fire beating and all-over sweat, her vision narrowing at the peripheries. On the other side of the door, in their bed, Thomas is waiting.

She comes into the room and turns away to change into her nightshirt.

Let me watch you, Thomas says. You're so beautiful with those breasts. Come to bed like that.

And she tells him, again, that the milk leaks, she's embarrassed about her still-soft stomach, she feels more attractive with less exposed.

I'll just look. You can put your shirt back on when we're done.

When we're done. And now the calculating, the series of *ifs* and *thens* she must go through, the urgency increasing with every night that passes since the last time they had intercourse. If she puts on the nightshirt now, after he's asked her to leave it off, he will roll over and turn out the light and go silent. If she says I'm sorry or Maybe tomorrow, he'll say Don't worry about it.

But when she opens her book, or turns on her lamp, he'll begin.

Why don't you want me anymore? Why can't I turn you on? It used to be easy.

And she will once again try to convince him that it's her fault, not his. Two babies, she'll say. Nursing hormones. I'm exhausted.

So stop nursing, he'll say. It's been four months. I want you back.

But she isn't ready to stop, she wants to breast-feed a full year. She cannot explain the desire to keep nursing, only that it's as insistent as an instinct. They will argue until it's time for her to get up and nurse again.

If she leaves the shirt off and comes to bed he will assume, because of this assent, that she would like him to *get her there*. He'll try things, tentative at first, gentle. And she will either pretend to enjoy what he's doing (what harm in pretending; as long as he comes, as long as she appears to come, they can both get a good night's sleep) or not pretend. If she decides not to pretend, he will either roll over and go silent or jerk off in front of her, his eyes on her breasts. He might put a finger inside before closing his eyes and disappearing into himself.

Or—the worst nights, the ones she's preparing herself for, in the bathroom—he will become someone she doesn't recognize.

Fuck this, he'll say when she gets into the bed with her shirt on. I want to be inside you, I'm your fucking husband— and he will shove her onto her side, then onto her stomach, the weight of his body pressing her into the mattress.

What is the least damaging path? Her body isn't hers anyhow, a toddler and an infant attached like appendages.

If she allows this—if she breathes through it till it's over—
they'll avoid a fight. She'll get some sleep. And her pain is
a private one. Really, she thinks, what is pain in this case?
Discomfort is the word for what her body feels. The pain
is spiritual, a chink in her soul each time she allows him to
penetrate, after all the refusals. But isn't it a loving thing, in
the end, to give him this? A soul-enriching thing, to satisfy
a husband, a good man and father who has never intention-
ally hurt her, or anyone?

She has a friend whose husband suffers with premature
ejaculation; another whose husband is addicted to porn.
Thomas has abandonment issues, she tells herself. It's a small
cross to bear.

It won't take long. She'll look at the books stacked on
her nightstand, the bottle of water, the ceramic lamp with
its taupe linen shade. When he's finished, he'll hold her and
stroke her hair and say, over and over, I'm sorry. That was the
last time. I swear to God, Maggie, it will never happen that
way again.

Take us to the Hyatt. In the backseat his fingers barely touching the edge of my thigh, taut in its pencil skirt. I began to shift my hips side to side—a fraction of an inch each way, the movement nearly imperceptible—side to side, over and over and the skirt began to ride up but he didn't move his hand so by the time we arrived at the hotel his fingertips were pressed against my skin. I stopped moving, he kept his hand where it was—this mutual refusal to pull away signifying our tacit agreement, *We will do the most we can do without the appearance of intent, we will do the most we can without speaking, without looking*, even my breath I kept as shallow as possible, as if word or look or breath would rupture some temporal membrane but as long as his hand stayed where it was, as long as my leg didn't move, we could stay here, poised between our platonic past and carnal future. Balanced on this precipice we could blow open eternity. The car idled. The driver cleared his throat. And then the indecision—the intentional nonaction—was over, James was pulling me out of the car, aggressively, by the elbow. I stood and tugged my skirt down, he gripped my wrist and said *Leave it*, in his eyes the amusement and admiration, but something else, too, what I'd seen in a priest's eyes once (attending mass with a Catholic friend; *Just do what I do*, she said), when he placed a wafer on my tongue and said, *Body of Christ broken for you*: sanctity, humility, willingness to be a vessel, used of God for a higher purpose. Also superiority and control. *For this I was ordained, there is no one else who can administer this sacrament, in this moment I am the only one who can give you what you need*, his fingers lacing into mine as he pulled me through the revolving doors behind him, so close that for a moment my hips were pressed into his backside and then we were in the lobby with its mirrors and modern fixtures, reception desks made of blocks of wood inlaid with marble, giant paintings like fractured stained glass. I gripped his hand, one solid thing in a universe quivering liquid. In the elevator I pressed floor 16, then moved to the back and let the mirrored wall hold me up. James stood beside me. The doors closed, our reflections slid into place: thin auburn-haired woman tall in heels; dark-headed, dark-suited man beside her. I watched the woman in the reflection lean against the man. Watched the man open his jacket and pull the woman against his white shirt.

Here is house. Here is red front door opening onto front staircase with a curved banister the husband wraps with colored lights each year at Christmas. A photo gallery that needs updating, school pictures of each child in uniform, polo shirts, khaki pants, and plaid skirts, in third grade the son wearing cowboy boots with his shorts, his hair slicked back with gel; daughter with a curly bob and bangs, hair lengthening and bangs growing out as the photos move up the stairwell. Here is dining room, farmhouse table pocked and gouged, the long mirror in which wife and husband and daughter and son have seen their reflections each day for nineteen years. Here is round kitchen table with four chipped-paint chairs, cat asleep on the window ledge, gerbil on a metal wheel, running for his life. Here is master bedroom with four-poster bed, king-sized mattress purchased after son was born. Dresser with its tiny top drawer in which wife has kept notes from children and husband and, tucked in an envelope, nude pictures of herself nine months pregnant. Here is bathroom, husband's idle razor, lidless bottle of cologne, engagement picture on a beach in San Diego, wife in a bandeau bikini, tanned skin and fifteen pounds lighter. Too thin, back then. Daughter's bedroom, twin beds ordered from Pottery Barn, carpet stained with paint, bulletin board with ticket stubs from movies and concerts, boarding passes from trips to England and India; handwritten Bible verses from when she used to go to Sunday school (*Let your beauty be that of your inner self*) and lists she made during her list-making phase—Things I Will Do This Summer: 1) dance in the rain 2) eat watermelon 3) watch the stars come out—each item with a small pencil drawing beside it. The monogrammed pillowcase she didn't take to college. Here is son's bedroom, stacks of books he never read, clear shoe boxes full of Legos and dominoes and marbles. Squirt guns, airsoft gun, Nerf gun, vestiges of a little boy's life.

Here is stove, microwave, coffeepot. The gravity of the kitchen sink. Here is window over sink, looking onto back porch and back door, through which wife has watched them leave, and come home, and leave again.

(How was Chicago? Thomas asks.

She's standing at the sink, holding a butter dish under hot running water.

Fine, she says. Busy.

Did you see that poet?

What poet?

The one at Princeton. The one you write to.

She turns off the water, places the butter dish facedown on the wooden drying rack.

Briefly, she says.)

I want you to list five positive and five negative memories from your childhood.

That isn't why I'm here.

Why are you here?

Because I fucked someone who isn't my husband. Because I'm in love with my husband. Because I'm in love with a man I can never speak to again. Because I want to stay married. Because I'm filled with longing for a life I can't have. Because I don't want to confess to Thomas. Because I must confess to Thomas.

I've been doing this for a long time, you need to trust me. Let's start with the memories.

But I want to talk about New York. How it was supposed to be the last time we ever saw one another. How the grief following that decision became fuel for what happened in Chicago.

Telling me about that day—and you've told me about it already—won't help the healing process.

We'll see about that.

I suppose we will.

September 11, 2016

New York City, overcast morning turning sunny and warm by afternoon, first edge of fall, angled sun and shadow on sidewalks and stoops. Everywhere, fire trucks, Never Forget signs, thank-yous, handshakes, hugs. We'd moved Tommy into his dorm at NYU two weeks before. Thomas had gone home to get back to work, I'd stayed on with a friend in Brooklyn.

I rode the F train from Carroll Gardens to West 4th. I'd planned to walk up 5th and meet James in Union Square. The summer heat was still trapped underground, stale air compressing my body, my feet so hot in my heels I took them off and walked barefoot through Washington Square Park, a carnival: a bearded man, shirtless and in socks, grabbing up pigeons and holding them to his mouth, one by one, though what he did with or to them was unclear, his long hair fell around his face and obscured the view. A man in a tuxedo playing *Clair de Lune* on a concert grand beside the fountain—he played badly, all rubato, no sense of the precision of the 9/8 time signature. A ballerina dressed as a dominatrix doing ronds de jambe for a cheering crowd, her long ponytail wrapped in a black cord. It kept smacking her face like a whip, leaving a red stripe across both cheeks. Pain obviously the salient part of her performance.

I walked under the arch—Empire State Building in front, Freedom Tower behind—glorious to be here, on this day, some new beat in my vascular system, an anticipatory cadence that matched the wider pulse of traffic and construction noise. *Life, life.* Manhattan was saying it. In the interstices between tragedies, the spaces between the arrowing buildings, the rush of air in alleyways and tunnels, breezes across rooftops, *life*. So much sweat and energy absorbed by the inanimate, I thought, if you removed every human from this island the stones would cry out. Faulkner said the East and Middlewest—New York, Chicago—are young because they're alive, the South old because it's dead. Killed by the Civil War. Maybe that was what I felt. I'd come up from Nashville to find myself among the living.

He hadn't been to the city on a 9/11 in the fifteen years since. Too painful, he said, too many souls lost. A colleague's mother, who worked in food services; a former classmate who worked in day care; the neurosurgeon who lived three doors down, whose newly graduated son worked at One World Trade Center. His second day on the job. He'd gotten a haircut, and that was the thing the surgeon noticed, James said, when he was called to identify the remains: the son's fresh haircut, precise edge along the neckline into which the surgeon pressed his face and wept.

James rode the train in from Princeton that Sunday to have lunch with his daughter at The New School, and to see me again, in the flesh. I imagined our parallel lives, when he described lunch with Caroline, her flyaway hair and the low-cut dress he kept wanting to adjust; my own daughter at Boston College, also a junior, with hair to her waist; and our sons, both starting their freshman years, with man-buns and habits of smoking weed in order to fall asleep at night. He'd made the requisite arrangements—though his wife wondered why, of all dates, he chose this one to go into the city—because I'd decided we should end our communication and he wanted to talk me out of it.

Did you tell Beth you'd see me? I asked. We were walking through Union Square.

I told her, he said. At the last minute.

And?

Tell Maggie I look forward to meeting her. That's what she said.

His phone chiming while I stopped to buy die-cut paper foldouts of the Taj Mahal for Kate, Eiffel Tower for Tommy; chiming as we walked up Broadway, making our way toward Penn Station so he could catch the train back. It was close to four. We looked at churches—Serbian Orthodox, Marble Collegiate—trying to find one with a door still unlocked, someplace cool and private. I bumped into an acquaintance crossing 28th. *Maggie?* she said. She was in the city en route from Amsterdam, had just been to India, where my daughter was about to go, and she told me how a shopkeeper in Delhi, wrapping a Ganesh statue in newspaper, complimented her choice: *You will not be disappointed, he is bestselling god!*

What are the odds, James said later, when we were sitting across from one another in a coffee shop. If you consider the number of people on this island.

The chimes were texts from his wife. *Why can't you get on an earlier train. We have the dinner tonight, I need you to pick up some wine. Caroline said you left her at two, what could you possibly have to talk about with Maggie for this long?* Texts finally superseded by a phone call. *I need a minute*, he said, putting the phone to his ear, and in the quick

way he said it—*I need a minute*—and more important what
the phrase meant (*Don't let Beth hear you while I've got her
on the line*), I wondered if I was one of many, just another
woman with whom he'd taken up a clandestine conversation, one more *frisson* fueled by lust and loneliness and the
need to tap into some kind of creative energy, some in-love-
ness, however fictitious, to keep him working; and if his wife,
knowing this pattern of his, was rightfully, mercifully insinu-
ating herself between us. I heard the edge of frustration in his
tone when he spoke to her, it was a response-in-kind, he was
only matching his pitch to her frustration and (deeper) fear,
as couples do; but I heard in his voice (Well, did they want us
there right at seven? Can I at least go home and change first?)
an impatience that, I imagined, would uncurl itself into full-
blown anger once he got home.

Sitting across from him, listening to his end of the conversation—beneath the table I was shredding my napkin, twirl-
ing the bits into pebbles—I imagined him explaining me to
his wife in the same tone. The buzz from the flirtation fuels
my art, she lives nine hundred miles away, what are you worried about?

She's fuel, nothing more, I imagined him telling his wife.

Though in the coffee shop that day I knew none of it was
true—knew, in his physical presence again, that whatever
was between us was dangerous, and real, and needed to end.

We can't just throw our friendship over a cliff, he said.
You've become too important to me.

I can't keep it up, I said. (Stuffing napkin-pebbles into my
jeans pocket.)

What are you afraid of, if we just keep up a professional dialogue?

That I'll keep being in love with you, I said. Hefted the word onto the table and let it sit there between us. Always my weakness, to lay out the unfiltered truth no matter the consequence. He looked away when I said the word love. Angry, maybe, that I'd said it first, or said it at all. (Two forces rule the universe, Simone Weil says. Light and gravity. And what is the reason that as soon as one human being shows he needs another, no matter whether his need be slight or great, the latter draws back? Answer: gravity.)

We finished our coffee and kept walking. At an intersection the light was changing; I started to run but he grabbed my elbow. Careful, he said, letting go and for three seconds pressing his palm between my shoulder blades, and in the afternoon glow of the fifteenth anniversary of 9/11 in New York City, a day on which nothing in the United States of America was *tangibly* amiss, I knew that our conversation, emails, shared music, photos, phone calls, texts, all of it would gather to a microscopic point, quivering with quantum energy, and if we decided to allow it—if we were brave or foolhardy or desperate or in love enough—would explode outward in a single, effortless, life-changing orgasm. I mean it was there for the taking if we wanted to take it. Even our bodies lined up, me lifted two inches in my heels so that when we turned to look at one another, standing at the intersection, we were eye to eye. Navel to navel, hip bone to hip bone.

We'd come up to it. Right up to the edge. I'd laid myself bare in front of him, made myself—what—too forward, distasteful? Though might it have been a way of trying to save myself, telling him I was in love? (And was I? Am I? Or is James—as you, Counselor, would say—the next in line, *my* line, a litany of men I draw toward myself not out of loneliness or unhappiness, but out of one desire, to be fucked by someone besides my husband? And because I only know arousal within love—because I've never separated emotion from body—is my pattern to create a pretend love first, over and over, in order to feel desire, and desirable?)

At the coffee shop we exchanged books. I gave him my marked-up copy of St. John of the Cross. In the absence of conversation, I said, this might be a way to feel as if we're still talking.

He gave me a Sharon Olds collection. This will break your heart, he said.

At 31st we cut over to 7th. We could try St. John the Baptist, he said.

In front of the church he looked at one last text.

I'm sorry but I have to run, he said.

And he did—he ran. Walking back downtown I fingered the napkin-pebbles in my pocket, then dropped them on the pavement. One by one, block by block. Leaving a trail in case he decided to turn around.

Maggie: Thank you for coming in to see me.

James: It was lovely—and lovely is the right word—to be with you in person again. Two years was too long. I only wish I didn't have to run off like that.

M: Probably for the best.

J: [. . . typing]

M: Though I'm feeling a bit melted now.

J: Are you in a cab?

J: Me too. Melted.

M: Yes. On Manhattan Bridge.

J: I'm going to write you tomorrow. A long letter.

M: [. . . typing]

J: I have more to say.

M: No. Let's let today be it.

J: Ok.

M: You read the book I gave you and I'll read the book you gave me.

J: Ok.

M: Thank you.

J: [. . . typing]

M: (heart)

J: (broken heart)

How clean, how simple the early days in the big house in Franklin. A house they will grow into. Green summer spilling into empty rooms, sunlight reflecting off wood floors, dust motes glittering like static. The back lawn sloping down to the wooden swing set and honeysuckle border; dogwoods and crape myrtles and pines along the driveway, their two cars parked beneath the trees. They intend to add on a garage but never get around to it. Over the years the hoods grow speckled with sap.

When the weather cools she opens the French doors and plays the grand piano—a Steinway, another inheritance purchase—imagining the notes carrying into neighbors' yards. The children are four and two. They press the keys of the upper register with their fingertips and Maggie lifts them into her lap, holds pointer fingers to press single notes. "Twinkle, Twinkle, Little Star," "Mary Had a Little Lamb." They run around naked after baths, hold hands and bounce on the bed. In the kitchen they pull out plastic containers with rainbow-colored lids.

Lellow, Kate says, handing a lid to Tommy.

Lellow, Tommy says.

Good job, little man! Kate says, kissing the top of his head.

Maggie doesn't correct Kate's backward-speak: godmother fairy, pale nolish, footbare, or the way she calls honeydew *greenalope*. While they nap Maggie wanders rooms, at peace with the tactility of child-rearing, the raw physicality of it. It's as if she's come to her senses outside of academia. She reads stories and novels, theology and poetry. And she writes poetry, or tries.

Potty training, sippy cups, half-day preschool, singsong videos. Now the children are five and three. They sit in tiny rocking chairs engraved with their names and watch a video her mother sent, an animated version of the Exodus story. The children love the songs, though she fast-forwards the scene in which the Angel of Death curls out of a cloud, a green vapor probing doorways, repelled by blood on lintels. They watch a series of videos called "Veggie Tales," put out by a nearby production company. A cucumber and tomato and other vegetables sing and act out stories from the Bible. "Dave and the Giant Pickle"; "Josh and the Very Big Wall"; "Where's God When I'm Afraid?" A tiny asparagus sings a song about God, and how he's bigger than the boogie man.

Foogie man, Tommy yells, foogie! Both children fall from their chairs, laughing.

Maggie hires a sitter so she can get groceries, go to the gym, sit in coffee shops with her notebook. Thomas has finished his MBA and is working for a private equity firm. Sometimes he comes home in the afternoons—an attempt to connect with her during nap time—before going back to work. He knows afternoons are her best time, the most-arousable hours. But it's startling, the abrupt shift in self-perception required, mommy to wife to lover. At night he wakes her, a hand on her breast or between her legs like a question. Why not? Tommy is long past nursing, we haven't made love in two weeks, why not?

The devolution into argument, or—more often—she'll roll onto her stomach voluntarily, looking at the spines of stacked books glowing in the dim night-light, and press up into him the way she knows he likes. He pulls out just before. Sometimes he cries, after. Sometimes she does too. Why can't married sex be easier? He's only satisfied if she reaches orgasm—something she can do only if she distances herself from him, in her mind, picturing another man and woman, imagining she is anywhere but there, in the bed beneath him. If she doesn't come it's as if he thinks he's failed in some way. He will need to try again the next night, and the next, until she can prove something with an orgasm. And then a few days' respite before the need starts up again.

He's a sieve, she thinks. No matter what I do—how I try to enjoy or move—it's never enough to satiate him, or convince him of . . . what? That he is adequate? That I won't leave him the way his mother did? Her climax—his ability to make her climax—is the sign and seal. *I am essential to Maggie.*

She wonders if she's to blame. At thirty-three Thomas is objectively beautiful. His thick hair has begun to silver all over, the rubble of his beard is still dark, the dent in his chin round as a shot. Set against his smooth skin, the silver hair and dark beard make him appear even younger than he is. Tall, athletic build, proportionate, his calves as developed as his chest and upper arms. She notices other women noticing him, wives of his friends. *Your husband looks like Patrick Dempsey,* one woman whispers to her, shyly, at a company dinner. She has the sense that in his presence women are ducking, lowering eyelids to look at him from beneath, almost subservient. She knows any one of them would love to sleep with him.

The panic is gone, the need to breathe in the bathroom. In its place is a strange lethargy. It's as if she's incapable of moving her limbs.

Thomas keeps a small towel beneath his side of the bed and is wiping her with it, gently, apologetically. He reaches for her hand; she lets him hold it. Inside her: negative space, apathy, the color gray.

After he's asleep—his hand on her upper arm and his foot touching her calf, maintaining connection—she lies awake and forces her brain to recollect. The conscious act of remembering, she's read, can have a sedative effect. And so she scrolls through the years: childhood, college with Thomas, the move to Princeton, the good years in grad school. Kate's birth, Tommy's, the move to Nashville. In her mind she watches them grow on fast-forward: two years old and newborn, three and one, four and two, five and three. Behind them, around them, a ruckus of books and toys and furniture. Physical systems tending toward states of disorder. Entropy, she thinks, is the trajectory of a household as it is the cosmos.

In August Kate starts kindergarten at a well-respected independent school. Each morning Maggie gathers Kate's long blond curls into a ponytail. She wears a uniform: navy polo and plaid skirt. The third week of school her new backpack arrives, printed with fall leaves and embroidered with her initials. Take a picture of me wearing it, Daddy! she says. Take one of me and Tommy! Tommy wears a makeshift loincloth, his legs stuck through the armholes of one of Thomas's T-shirts, excess fabric twisted up and pinned in place. He carries a wrapping-paper tube for a spear. The children pose, arms wrapped around one another, while Thomas snaps with a digital camera. Kate and Thomas leave together—he drops her off on his way in to work each day.

Maggie's getting Tommy ready for preschool when the woman who drives his car pool calls.

You heard it's canceled today, right? she says.

Canceled?

Preschool. Are you watching this?

Watching what?

Just turn on your TV.

Within minutes she sees the second plane hit. She takes Tommy upstairs to the playroom, puts on a video, and runs back downstairs. Alone and horrified, she watches both towers fall. She keeps calling Thomas but can't get through. He must know people. They must.

She buckles Tommy into the backseat and drives to the school, which is on lockdown. They wait in the parking lot, where other parents have gathered. Everyone stays inside cars, listening to radios. She doesn't turn hers on. She wants to pray but can't think of a single phrase that sounds right. A beautiful morning, sunny and warm, light and sky mirrored in the school's arched front window.

The children emerge. Teachers and aides walk them to waiting cars. Kate climbs into the backseat, her eyes wide.

The TV was on and I saw *black smoke,* she says. Miss Gifford turned it off and said sit in the hallway and draw how we feel.

She hands Maggie her drawing: a girl with pigtails and giant tears falling in straight lines to the bottom of the page.

Lemme see, Tommy says.

A airplane flew into a *building,* Tommy! Kate says.

Where? Tommy looks out the window.

It's far away, it's the Empire State Building, Kate says.

Thomas comes home at lunch, hugs them all.

No one I know yet, he says. Phone lines are down. My God, Maggie.

The children pull out snow boots and the vacuum hose and carry them into the backyard. From the open kitchen windows she watches them play firemen. They take turns being the rescuer, dragging one another by the wrists through the long grass.

Pretend you're stuck, Kate says to Tommy. Pretend you can't breathe.

Before nap time, Maggie gets the American flag out of the hall closet. Together, she and Kate and Tommy carry it down the driveway and slide it into the bracket on the doll-house-shaped mailbox left by the previous owner. She's been meaning to order a new mailbox, something plain, but the children beg her to keep it. A Lego family lives inside. Maggie finds them in various setups when she gets the mail: sitting around a flat rock like a table, or lying in a row, covered with bits of paper towel.

In his loincloth Tommy perches on the rock landscape wall, spear in hand, surveying the weedy lawn and shaded street. Kate picks dandelion puffs and blows off the seeds. The sun slants through the twinkling maple leaves. Breeze, birdsong, the stark blue of sky. Impossible.

See if I like butter, Kate says, holding up a dandelion. Maggie twists the flower on Kate's chin, tilts her small face left and right to inspect.

Ah, Maggie says. Neon yellow. You *love* butter.

Do butter to me! Tommy says. Maggie bends to press the flower into his uplifted chin.

Why are you crying? he asks her.

Because I feel sad, Maggie says.

About the people on the airplanes? Kate asks, frowning.

Yes. And their families.

Those people didn't *die,* Kate says. They flew up to heaven.

Watch this, Tommy says, jumping off the rock ledge.

I saw them going up, on the TV, Kate says, insistent, almost angry. I saw them floating in the sky. Mommy. Stop crying.

June 2017

Dear James:

Sometimes, when I'm home alone, I listen to myself repeat our dates aloud, like a litany:

Nashville, July 2014
New York, September 2016
Chicago, April 2017

(Lord, lamp unto my feet and light unto my path—how is it possible?)

I'm still reading the blue book. It's painful, the way she writes about loss. I can only take it in small amounts. The ancients, she says, disagreed as to whether we perceived objects, or objects perceived us. Do our eyes throw out a beam, like a lantern, that illuminates them? Or do the objects send out rays which, reaching our eyes, reveal them to us—as if they're looking back? Plato, she writes, split the difference: a visual fire burning between the eye and the object it beholds.

   I cannot help applying these ideas to love. Its location in a physical sense. Was it something we carried in ourselves— something I sent out to you, and you sent out to me? Or did it exist independently, a *potential* fire hovering in the middle space between us, appearing only when we looked at one another? In which case, the second we stopped looking, the fire disappeared. Hence my use of the past tense. (But dear God I want to use the present. I want to keep looking, to *gaze at length*. I want access, again—hours, days, months— to memorize the side-sweep of his smooth hair, the freckles on his legs, the tiny mole on his nipple. I want to sit on top of him and study the veins in his cock; to imagine, over and over, the particular angle at which he held it the moment he lifted my hips from behind and bent into my torso, me with the stacked pillows beneath my hips, waiting—put his mouth against my ear and said, *Hold still, this might hurt.*)

One of the spines on my nightstand: *Letters of John Newton*. Earmarked page: *Various Uses of Temptation in the Life of the Believer*. But who is John Newton? I must familiarize myself with his story, if I'm to glean from him anything worthwhile regarding the nature of temptation. Which I must. Glean from him what is worthwhile regarding what happened at the Hyatt, in order to repent, accept forgiveness, forgive myself. Love my husband and children with integrity.

Above all, to stop missing you.

Newton: born in London, 1725. Mother died when he was seven. Became a mariner at the age of eleven, went to sea with his father, lived aboard ships until his stroke at thirty. In the intervening years he became a slave trader. Likely impregnated slave women on the ship in order to sell them at a premium upon arrival in port. Libertine, infidel, injurious, old African blasphemer—words he applied to himself. Then: his Great Awakening. Conversion and settlement in the parish at Olney, where he famously wrote hymns with the depressed Cowper. *Amazing Grace, How Sweet the Name of Jesus*

Sounds. A wretch, once lost, who tells me what temptation is useful for:

1. *To show me what is in my heart.*

   Burning. Ear is burning sounds are burning nose is burning odors are burning tongue is burning flavors are burning body is burning tangibles are burning. Mind, idea, consciousness, burning. Burning with what? With lust, and delusion.

2. *To make me sensible of my immediate and absolute dependence upon God.*

   "Whom have I in heaven but you? And earth has nothing I desire besides you." Asaph, Psalm 73. This is not my truth anymore. Though I ask you to make it so, God. May Earth have nothing—no one—that I desire. Grant me estrangement. Ear, nose, tongue, body. Outward forms, mind, idea.

3. *To conform me to Christ in his sufferings: "Can you wish to walk in a path strewed with flowers when his was strewed with thorns?"*

   But did Christ experience sexual temptation? Adulterous, homoerotic, pedophiliac, bestial? We are told he was tempted in every way but was without sin. Yet according to Christ himself to even imagine a sin is to commit the sin itself. Ergo: How was he tempted without imagining the temptation? Why even use the word temptation? Is this a translation issue?

4. *That I might sympathize with my suffering brethren, and be able to speak a word in season to them that are weary. "If your prayers, your conversation, and the knowledge others have of your trials afford them some relief in a dark hour, this is an honor and privilege which, I am persuaded, you will think you have not purchased too dear, by all you have endured."*

In a dark hour. Here we are, then, in New York City, looking for a cathedral with a door left open, someplace more private than a coffee shop, a cool interiority where we might sit or kneel or lie prostrate and pray aloud together. Low-burning candles, icons, statues, perhaps an empty confessional into which we could steal and enact the roles of penitent and priest and say to one another, through the grate, with the safety of a wall between us, the things we said in room 1602 at the Hyatt, postcoital and sweaty on the soft beige carpet. The things you told me to say when we did it again on the bed. Perhaps, had we found such a space prior to that night in Chicago—a dark hour in which to confess to one another the nature of our temptation, the dreadful joy of the crush, how we became aroused by, and secretly masturbated to, one another's written words and images, and the lies we told our spouses (just a friend, a colleague really); had we analyzed, together, the stance of friends (side by side looking ahead to a shared horizon) versus lovers (side by side looking at one another) and admitted that, yes, we had turned, we were no longer looking forward—perhaps then I might have said, Pray for me, I'm tempted by you. You might have said the same to me. And then—what? Would we have allowed ourselves to do, inside a church, what we did in Chicago? What might have happened, had we done those things in a sacred space? I imagine statues beginning to weep, blood curling down the carved marble ankles on the crucifix above the altar, *For this moment I died, for this moment I am always dying, every moment for all eternity I am bleeding so they can sit in the pew in this sanctuary and allow their fingertips to touch on the wooden bench, allow themselves to hold hands in an attempt to pray, then turn toward one another, he sliding a hand inside the ripped knee of her jeans to feel the skin of her thigh and musculature of her quadriceps (see the human machinery on which I am eternally pushing myself up to draw a breath), she reaching her hand beneath his jacket, running it over the smooth cotton of his checked shirt (see the sword-pierce just below my own bare chest).* Which of us would have noticed the bleeding Christ, the inclined head and glassy forsaken gaze into eternity, the stench of hell? Which of us would have pulled back and said, but the suffering! We cannot forget the suffering! You would say, We have beautiful families, we cannot cause them pain. I would say, We can endure our own pain but we must never consummate this—my hand inside your shirt, index finger tracing a line down your abdomen, the sparse soft hair; your fingers unfastening the buttons on my blouse.

The third day. That is what we'd be thinking. *The resurrection that follows suffering, no condemnation for those who are in Christ Jesus* (lips, mouths, tongues, hands, burning) *why not go on sinning so that grace may increase?*

The doors were locked. Every church we tried.

They're never left open, he said outside St. John the Baptist, because of the homeless.

Neither of us insensible of the irony: we were shut out because of the very people who should be let in.

On her thirty-second birthday Thomas brings home an unmarked cardboard box.

Keep an open mind, he says.

Inside the box, in Bubble Wrap, is a flesh-colored vibrator. Realistic-looking, veined and arched, a switch at its base. Bigger than Thomas.

It's supposed to be the one that's closest to real, he says.

But why? Maggie says.

I'm the only man you've ever been with, he says. This is a safe way for you to experience something different.

She leaves it in the box and puts it inside a suitcase beneath her side of the bed, where the children won't find it. And when he asks—*Can we try, here, you run it under hot water*—the first time she holds it against her skin, it's as if she's withdrawing into herself, away from Thomas and reality.

Can you, he breathes. I mean, will you—if it feels okay—

She's lying on her back, he's kneeling beside her on the bed, watching from above. She inserts just the tip. Pushes a bit farther, arching to get the angle right. Thomas makes a choked sound, falls onto her, shudders. The tentative wiping-off with a towel. She grabs it from him and does it herself.

You didn't like it, he says.

It's an object, she says. I don't have an emotional connection to an object.

I know, he says. But for me to watch, I mean it's so—

Don't ask me to do that again.

I'll get rid of it right now, he says, stuffing it into the box.

At night they hear Kate's voice hours after they've put the children to bed. Maggie goes upstairs and finds her sitting cross-legged in the dark.

Everything okay up here? Maggie asks.

I'm talking to my friends in heaven, Kate says.

What friends?

Just some girls. Actually one's a boy.

Maggie sits on the edge of the bed.

What are their names?

They won't tell me.

What do you and your friends talk about?

They ask me questions. Only now they stopped because you're here.

Can you remember what you were talking about, just now?

Something about a cat, she says.

Kate begins to cry every night at bedtime, saying she's scared to go to sleep. One night, when Thomas switches off her lamp, she throws up on her quilt. She starts to throw up after dinner, as soon as she starts thinking about bedtime. Thomas and Maggie take turns lying on the floor beside her until she's asleep. She wakes up in the middle of the night and comes downstairs to get into bed with them.

My friends won't talk to me, she says, her thin body quivering.

Let's let her sleep in our room until she's out of this phase, Maggie says the next morning.

I don't know. Won't it feed things, to cater to her fear?

The following week Maggie takes Kate in for a haircut.

The stylist comes to the waiting area a few minutes after she's shampooed Kate's hair.

I'd like to show you something, the stylist says.

Kate's curls are wet and combed flat. From the back of her head sprouts what looks like the tip of a tiny saguaro cactus.

We have a little breakage back here, the stylist says, chipper.

Where? Kate says, a hand flying to the back of her head.

Have you been pulling your hair, Katie bug? Maggie says.

Sometimes, Kate says. I promise I won't do it anymore.

Her grandmother's basement in Cleveland: the magic of looking up to the ground. At the foot of the staircase, galoshes and coats and shovels and a cupboard beneath the stairs, big enough for all three grandchildren—Maggie, Sarah, and Steven—to hide in. A pool table, old records, dozens of jars, most empty, some with buttons or spools; a half-done puzzle of a red barn at sunset, cows in the foreground. *Life* magazines, Band-Aid tins with Cracker Jack prizes inside, shoe boxes with hardened photographs, all the horrified doomed ancestors. On a pedestal table, hatboxes containing lacy fascinators, plates filled with jeweled brooches and gaudy clip-on earrings. What woman wore these things? Surely not her grandmother. And Uncle Rick, her father's brother, who used to be in a band—upstairs he sat, in front of the television, watching football, the fat bald uncle who never married and smelled of Ben-Gay. His only way of relating to his nieces and nephew was to buy them presents, or stick out his arm and let them hang from it like a monkey bar. Was he the thin man in these photos, dark hair slicked back, wearing a white suit and lurching into the microphone, like Elvis?

Uncle Rick never married because he fell in love with a black woman, Maggie's mother told her once. Your grandma wouldn't let the woman inside the house. He didn't have the guts to choose her over his own mother. Try not to fault Grandma, it's how things were back then.

The basement smelled of laundry detergent and cedar mixed with wet wood and mothballs. Life and decay in coexistence. Above the washing machine was a laundry chute, out of which tumbled toys and books, sent by her siblings from floors above. In the attic three floors up Sarah would whisper into the chute and it was as if she were speaking directly into Maggie's ear. Anything was possible in this house. She could float down her grandmother's stairs: attic to bedrooms, bedrooms to living room, living room to basement. So many stairs, nothing like the flat houses in Phoenix. Some impulse—a flutter of nerves in her stomach—and she would drift down to the next landing, her feet never touching the steps.

At home, too, lying in bed at night, she could hover on a horizontal plane above her mattress. A lovely feeling, warm and silent, as if she were suspended in thick gel. She knew the gel was God, he was all around yet nowhere she could see— outside the planet in the stars and also inside it, in the ball of burning lava. God was in the spangled light at the bottom of the swimming pool; he was in the shifting sun and shadows on the white-painted brick wall in her bedroom, a film of pure motion, the patterns like a code or language she felt always on the cusp of understanding. He was in the circles that spun on the backs of her eyelids when she tried to fall asleep and in the glowing visions of bodies of water appearing and disappearing, swelling and drying up.

Sometimes, with her eyes shut tight, she saw a head circled in thorns, too close to glimpse the face before it disappeared.

God wasn't inside the church—a low brick building with potted palms in the foyer and orange-cushioned pews in the sanctuary. Inside the church people didn't act the way adults were supposed to act. They cried, or made typewriter sounds with their teeth, their hands stretched out like they wanted something. It was as if they'd forgotten who they were: her father's partner, the principal at her school, the lady who worked at the country club snack bar. A retarded teenage boy with sweaty hands liked to touch her hair. Let him do it, her mother said, children like that are God's angels, they bless us with their touch. Sarah and Steven would run away when they saw the boy, so she had to be the one to stand still. Pretty, the boy would repeat, his moist hand swirling on her scalp.

At the end of the sermons the people would sing *Just as I Am* until a man in waders appeared in the little Jacuzzi above the altar. Any man could baptize someone, not just the preacher. The man in waders would push a person backward, underwater. Amen, amen! people would yell. She would never do such an embarrassing thing. Jesus had been embarrassed for her. He'd been naked and whipped and everyone had seen it. Why should she have to be embarrassed too?

It's a way to show our love and gratitude, the Sunday school teacher said. To be a little embarrassed. To go under, and come up again – a *painless* participation in Christ's death, burial, and resurrection.

One night she heard a voice outside her window, terrifying, as loud as a train roaring through her bedroom, or all the drums and cymbals in an orchestra sounding at once. *Little Girl.* The voice sounded exasperated, like a babysitter who was sick of playing games and wanted to watch TV. She ran through the dark house into her parents' bedroom and stood by her father's side of the bed.

A man's outside my window, she said.

Sarah? Her father's deep voice, a puff of stale breath beside her face.

It's Maggie, she said. The man said *Little girl*.

You were dreaming, he said.

No I wasn't. I heard him. He yelled it through my window.

Maggie? Her mother's voice, from the other side of the bed. Come snuggle for a while.

July 2017

Dear James,

If you and I were still in contact, I would write to tell you about the visions I've been having. Photographic negatives on the backs of my eyelids, arriving at the edges of sleep, as they did when I was a child. Likely the images are a by-product of the fact that I haven't been able to sleep much since Chicago. Or else the intellect's attempt to create a dark narrative around us. To convince myself it's right, in the sight of God—and according to our agreement, and to the tenets of basic human decency—to no longer be in contact with you.

Head giving Heart what it needs. Head saying to Heart, *The two of you, together, are wrong.*

Still the visions come.

1. A hawk at the bottom of its dive, talons extended; *the slow-motion, downward beat of wings.* When Tommy left for college I bought six pullets. All the years of daily caretaking finished, and all I wanted was something to take care of, daily. The chicks were pecking around beneath the azaleas. I sat in the grass nearby to make sure they didn't wander to the neighbor's yard. The day was warm. I lay back and fell asleep and woke just in time to see a flurry of white feathers. No, I yelled, standing and waving my arms. No no no. The hawk dropped the chick and, unharmed, it ran to join the others beneath the bushes. How long had the hawk been

perched in the trees, honing in? Waiting for me to be still long enough to mean I was no longer a threat?

2. A snake-faced man in a graveyard, at night, finds out his plans have been thwarted by some ultimate good. He turns on his heel, *long cloak flaring out behind him.* I admit this cloaked figure bears a resemblance to Ralph Fiennes as Voldemort in the Harry Potter films. (There was also, in the vision, a clawlike hand, bent fingers cradling a wand.) But it was the sense of the man's anger that came across in the vision, his fierce intention to redouble whatever evil efforts were under way. Understand: this man isn't you. The flare of cloak as he turns on his heel is an image of some dark intention behind us—the thing that wanted, and maybe still wants, to destroy me, and you, and our families.

3. A tree limb penetrates a windshield as the driver is doing 45 on a two-lane highway; an explosive sound, *glass like sugar coating the driver's skin.* This one isn't a vision in the technical sense. You might remember when it happened, I wrote to you about it. Looking back I realize I should have seen it as a warning. It rained the day before and the hillside trees with their shallow root systems were saturated. I was on the phone with Kate, who was telling me what she wanted from the taco truck, and then a tree was hanging in front of me, upside down, as if dangling from the sky by its roots. The limb through the windshield was ten inches around. As the

EMTs duct-taped the glass dust off my sweaty skin—it was Labor Day, I'd just come from the gym—the police officer who took the report walked around and around the car.

So you didn't swerve to avoid it, he said.

No, I said, wanting to explain that in the split second between tree-dangle and limb-pierce, a little eternity opened up during which I was able to almost leisurely evaluate the situation. Swerve right and hit the hillside, swerve left and risk a head-on collision, let the tree hit and give yourself the best odds.

Six inches to the right and you'd of had a limb through your skull, the policeman said.

When I wrote to tell you about the wreck, I wanted you to call and say—what? *Get on a plane, let's not waste any more time? I'm coming to see you, life is precarious, we should be together?*

I'm glad you're okay, you wrote. Then shared a short history of your own car wrecks, one involving a school bus with a football team on board.

Last week I wrote on my wrist, in a superfine Sharpie, in a tiny cursive script that only I could read: *wings, cloak, sugar.* To fortify my resolve to never contact you again.

What's that on your wrist? Thomas asked.

Just a few things I need to pick up at the market, I said.

One day, while the children are at school—Kate in third grade, Tommy in first—she goes into the bedroom and sees the cat pawing a string hanging from the edge of her pillow. Beneath the pillow she finds a drawstring bag with a tiny pink pebble vibrator inside, delicate, shaped like a kidney bean. She presses the button at its base, presses it again; the vibration quickens and changes pattern.

At the bottom of the bag is a note from Thomas: *This one's just for you. Try it? And—if you like it—maybe we can use it together?*

God wants your holiness, not your happiness—this from a sermon in her parents' church. All of history, the pastor said, is one long terrible story of men and women trying to make themselves happy. They try so many things. Nothing works. They cry out to God: Can you please give me something to make me happy? And God says: I give you Myself. Yes, yes, they say, but give me something tangible, something with skin on it! And God says: Unless you have me, I have nothing to give.

At least three times a month, the pastor continued, an unhappy spouse would come to his office and say, This marriage can't be God's will for me. God wants me to be happy.

And the pastor would say, Show me where it says that in the Bible.

Uncomfortable laughter, a hand pulled through hair.

I mean it, the pastor would say, sitting back as if to wait the person out. Open the Bible and show me the verse.

Maggie and Thomas sit on the therapist's couch with Kate between them. Thomas clears his throat over and over. Dr. Pierson is tall, skinny, with a full dark beard and rimless glasses. He sits in a chair across from them, wearing a T-shirt, jeans, and Puma sneakers. His office is like a living room: couches and chairs, a coffee table with a bowl holding chocolate kisses and peppermints. Toys, Harry Potter books, a game console.

So, Miss Kate, Dr. Pierson says. I hear you've been having some thoughts that are bossing your body around.

Kate is silent. Dr. Pierson doesn't look at Maggie or Thomas. He reaches for a book, flips through the pages, holds it up.

Have you read any of these yet?

Not that one, Kate says. I just saw the movie, though.

Which book is your favorite so far?

I don't know.

You liked the first one a lot, remember? Thomas says. The one I read to you, with the owls?

They all have owls, Kate says.

Dr. Pierson pulls a plastic figurine from his pocket and hands it to Kate.

Do you know who that is?

Lupin, she says.

Do you remember when he turned into a werewolf? That part scared me. And it scared my son, who's twelve. Did it scare you?

Kate nods.

Let's say you had a movie-theater clicker. Would you have wanted to change the channel?

I just closed my eyes, Kate says.

I want you to try something, Dr. Pierson says. I want to show you how you can make your own channel inside your head. What's the cutest thing you can think of?

Baby rabbit.

Your favorite color?

Blue.

Okay. I want you to close your eyes and look at a tiny blue rabbit. She's so fluffy you can hardly see her little eyes in all that fur. She's sitting in a basket. The basket is attached to a giant rainbow-striped hot air balloon. I want you to watch her float up in the balloon. Not very high, just above the grass. She's peeking over the edge of the basket. Her eyes are wide and her blue ears are sticking straight up. You with me?

Kate nods.

Now—this is the part where you have to be brave—I want you to change the channel. I want you to picture the scene in the Azkaban movie, where Lupin's a werewolf and his mouth is open and you can see all his sharp teeth. I want you to really look at him. His mouth might be getting closer to you. Tell me when you see him.

I see him.

Good. Now—quick—go back to the baby rabbit.

You can open your eyes, Kate, Dr. Pierson says. I'm going to ask you some questions. You don't have to answer anything you don't feel like answering. How did you feel when you were watching the baby rabbit?

Happy I guess.

What about your body? Did you notice anything about how your arms or your hands or your mouth felt? Your eyes or throat or tummy?

Kind of peaceful?

Peaceful. That's a great word. What about when you saw Lupin?

Scared. Only a little.

Did you notice your arms or hands or face feeling any different?

Not really. Maybe kind of stiff?

Guess what. You know everything there is to know about doing my job now. Because all I do is help people understand how things they think in their *heads* and things they feel in their *bodies* are connected.

I'm pretty confident you're going to get this last question right, Dr. Pierson says. When the channel changed, who was holding the remote control?

Me, Kate says.

And we have a winner, ladies and gentlemen, Dr. Pierson says. You can change the channel in your head anytime you have thoughts that start to boss your body around. We just need to spend a little time together, practicing.

When the session is over, Dr. Pierson tells Kate she can play a video game while the adults wrap up the boring stuff in the waiting room.

Anxiety's incredibly common in precocious children, Dr. Pierson says. Their imaginations take them down roads their bodies aren't equipped to navigate. I'd like to start with bio-feedback exercises. No meds for now.

Also, he says, I always ask this, so please don't take it personally: anything else going on at home I should know about?

August 2017

Dear James:

There was a fourth vision. This one doesn't show me any darkness. But it was the same as the other three—vivid, insistent—so I don't know how to weigh it.

I was on the plane at LaGuardia, the day after I saw you in New York. We were twelfth in line for takeoff. I closed my eyes and pressed my face into the window and, against the darkness of my eyelids, saw the city divested of all its buildings but three: Freedom Tower at the bottom, Empire State in the middle, and at the top, somewhere in the Bronx, an enormous crucifix, as tall as the island was long. Had the cross been a human the Freedom Tower would have reached to its knees. While I watched, the cross lay itself down over Manhattan. Just bent forward and fell. The horizontal beam became a pair of arms and wrapped the island up, as if the cross were hugging a pillow to its chest. Manhattan curled in on itself. *This much love.* I don't want to say I heard the words, but I felt them, a bass note throughout my body. *All the mess and glory of this city, and still this much. And you, with your wayward thoughts, in the agony of temptation: I would have you no other way.* Yet how to reconcile the other visions of the evil behind our situation—judgment, requisite obedience to an impossible standard—how do I balance these with this glimpse of unconditional love and infinite mercy? Who would make up such a contradictory religion? If there is such a thing as Divine truth surely it would come to us transposed in this way, revealing the inadequacy of our brains to comprehend (we must hold A and not-A to be true simultaneously), and in so revealing our intellectual limitations, prove itself "true" beyond such binary categories as "true" or "false."

Or maybe the complexity is simply the human brain just before insanity, functioning at the peak of its evolutionary capabilities. No more black and white, everything gray. And then we disappear. A virus wiped from the planet.

W*hat if you woke one day to discover the corpse of Christ had been identified definitively? Or that an irrefutable, airtight scientific study had been devised to disprove the existence of God, and the study had—beyond any conceivable doubt—proved he did not exist? What would you feel?*

Relief.

One evening in the fall, after Kate has been seeing Dr. Pierson for a few months, Thomas carries into the kitchen a television-sized box with holes in the lid. He sets it in the center of the table; the box jiggles and whines.

Maggie has just taken the children to the market. On the table are pumpkins, carving kits; an army helmet, tiara and wand; camouflage face-paints, bags of candy.

What do you think is inside? he asks the children.

Tell us!

You have to guess.

Puppy, kitten, bunny, tell us!

Thomas opens the lid and lifts out a black Lab, eight weeks old. It pees on the table, tail wagging.

Look how excited he is, Maggie says.

Can I hold him? Kate is half-crying. Can I *name* him?

He's going to sleep in your room at night, Kate, Thomas says. Let's let Tommy name him.

I want him to sleep in my room, Tommy says.

You get to walk him, Tommy, his father says. That's going to be your special job.

Thomas sets the puppy on the kitchen floor; his paws are huge, they splay out. Flat on his belly, he sniffs and licks vigorously at a spot on the hardwood.

Duncan's cat's named Wiggins, Tommy says. He's black too.

Here, Wiggins, Thomas says. Watch, if you rub butter on your hand he'll lick it right off.

In the trunk of his car is a dog crate, still in pieces. Thomas puts it together and Maggie helps him carry it up to Kate's room. Kate is sitting on her bed, blue comforter gathered into her lap, the puppy asleep in the little nest she's made inside her crossed legs.

Why does he have to sleep in a cage? Kate asks.

It's so he doesn't have an accident, Maggie says. When he's house-trained he can sleep in bed with you.

Here's my elephant blankie, Tommy says, running in with his baby blanket.

Want to sleep in my room tonight, Tommy? Can Tommy sleep in my room?

They put the puppy in the crate and the children arrange Tommy's blanket in the corner. Together they sit in front of the crate with their hands inside.

Go to sleep, Wiggins, Kate says. Tommy, hand me that book. No, the one with the mouse on front.

Kate reads to the puppy over whines and yips, until he circles and collapses on the blanket.

It might be just the thing, Maggie says that night, in bed.

I had a dog at her age, Thomas says. I don't know why I didn't think of it sooner.

It's genius, she says.

He rolls to face her and puts a hand under her shirt.

Have you tried it yet? he asks.

I haven't wanted to.

We've got to try something.

Maybe if we just talked.

God damn it, Maggie, I'm trying.

Later, after she's rolled onto her side and made the kinds of noises she knows will help (What harm in pretending?

What harm?); after Thomas has pushed into her so hard she cried out with the pain, and he pushed harder, thinking she liked it; after he's finished on the sheets and told her, shoulders shaking, that he's sorry, and she has said no, she enjoyed it; after he has begged her not to leave him, and promised, again, that he will wait, he won't ask her to use anything, he will offer only his own skin, his own flesh and blood (*Let's throw the pebble away,* he'd said, *let's wrap it up in a kitchen bag and put it outside in the dumpster*)—when all of this is over and Thomas is finally asleep beside her and she's filled with the gray numbness, only then does she think to pray, a poem she remembers approximately: *Dear God, who are my rock my steady Christ, hear me. I lie here lost hidden pushed away from the core. Endanger me, if not in my body then by words hammered into my brain, or death as fire, as slow flaying, as bloody lilies. But not this nothing.*

October 2017

Dear James,

It's been six weeks since I took out this journal. Which also means it's been six weeks since I've prayed.

The blue author (I wouldn't bring her up so often if I were actually sending these letters) writes about "nostalgia for samsara." Longing for the past, our own or someone else's—in the Buddhist tradition, a source of *dukkha*, the Sanskrit word in the first of the Four Noble Truths that is most often translated as "suffering," but is closer in meaning to dissatisfaction. This nostalgia-suffering has a noble purpose: It alerts us to our attachment to the illusion of the birth-death-rebirth cycle. The importance of escaping the burning wheel of samsara. *Yet the talons of attachment seem to sharpen,* she writes, *as soon as we begin to understand the need to escape them.*

When the talons of attachment dig in, I remind myself that the act of remembering changes the thing remembered. That I've replayed what happened in Chicago so often, the night has become wholly my own invention. Who was it that said if someone gave her flowers, she would arrange them in a vase with no water, give them a good hard look, then put them in the back of her closet? That she couldn't wait for them to die so she could enjoy remembering them?

C. S. Lewis says that if we were able to return to the locus of our nostalgia, the place or person or spot of time in which we experienced joy, we would find only more nostalgia. As far back as we could go—a view from a childhood window, patterned light on a nursery wall—we would find only an unsatisfied desire that is itself more desirable than any other satisfaction. An indication not of the *illusion* of our existence, but of its ultimate reality elsewhere. A home we once knew but can't quite remember, to which we will someday return.

I try to hold these two views in balance. Buddhist, Christian. Impossible. One ends in Nirvana, nonbeing; the other in personal, individual resurrection. The Christian idea of an afterlife in which we all still exist as individuals, but together, as a body—our ancestors, children, grandchildren, friends, every soul we've touched, and they've touched, and every soul those people have touched, and so on, some grand knitting-together of persons, each still him or herself but in a new, completed, interconnected way—I mean, it sounds nice. It sounds like a child telling her mother she's got friends in heaven.

But the other idea. Extraction from the talons. What relief there would be in no longer longing to feel, again, your whiskers on my inner thighs.

She pretends the swimming pool is a grave. Allows her body to sink and lies, faceup, eyes open, on the bottom of the shallow end. Compression in her ears, burning in her lungs, the sky above still visible but changed in the wavering gradations of blue and white. Weight of water a benign scrim between worlds. In bed at night, too, she imagines dying: the sudden drop of her legs down into the mattress, the waking jerk back to horizontal. Dying will be just so, she tells herself. Nothing scary about it. Her legs will drop, her feet will find some new solid ground beneath them, and she will simply stand.

You consider this—imagining your own death—a positive childhood memory?

Yes.

You weren't frightened by the thought of dying?

Not when I was a child.

Do you remember when you first became afraid?

I'm not sure. Around the time I got pregnant with Kate.

Do you remember other times, since?

On the way home from the hospital, after the C-section with Tommy. On an airplane to London. In the hotel room with James.

What were you afraid of, specifically, in each instance?

That we would get into a wreck and the seat belt would split my stitches and I would bleed to death before the ambulance arrived. The fall from the sky into the ocean, those final moments of terror, knowing what was about to happen and being powerless to stop it. That if I died that night, in the hotel room in Chicago, my family would find out. That what was happening that night would never happen again.

Let's talk about Chicago.

I can't. Not yet.

At some point you're going to have to.

To tell you what happened will strip the memory of its power. Bleed some of the color out.

Isn't that what you want? Why you keep talking to me? To find some release from the suffering of loss, to continue on in your marriage with perspective?

Yes. Yes to all of that—

So: you arrived at the hotel after the aborted film . . .

And it was sad. Depressing really. We undressed in front of one another and, naked, could only think about the fact that each of our spouses had seen our younger, more muscular selves. I kept one arm beneath my breasts to lift them, the other hand over the patch of hair; he kept his arms crossed over the paunch of his stomach. A brief kiss and we put our clothes back on and watched *Seinfeld* reruns until we fell asleep.

Actually I was the aggressor. I don't know where it came from, I've never been that way with Thomas. I pushed him onto his back and straddled him so hard he winced. *Careful,* he kept saying, *careful, I have a slipped disk.*

Actually he entered me three ways at once. Cock in my mouth, tongue in my front, fingers in my back. Turned me over and pulled my hips up so he could enter another way—*I don't want the part of you Thomas has had, I want what's untouched*—and I cried from the burn, guttural sobs he ignored until he finished and turned me over again and stopped my sobbing with his mouth. Afterward I begged him to do it again that way, I mean I *welcomed* the pain as an appropriate manifestation of the betrayal we were bringing into the world that night, a small-scale version of the brokenness we were creating, in ourselves if we kept the affair a secret, in our spouses if we confessed, and in our children, grandchildren, friends, and coworkers and every fucking person who'd known and admired our long-lasting marriages over the years.

Actually it was otherworldly, ecstatic in a religious sense, at the deepest point of penetration the room fell away and

the sky tore open and we were swept up into electric galaxies, our bodies fused together in the presence of a God who
allowed us to reach up and run our fingers through the down
of his beard . . .

Enough. I can see you're not ready for this.

(But God, God, tall friend of my childhood, you saw everything that night. How I began crying in the elevator, his jacket half-wrapped around me. Kept crying as we undressed. My legs wouldn't stop shaking, I couldn't make it to the bed, just sank to the floor in my bra and underwear while he lay beside me and touched my face and, with an almost unbearable tenderness, finished undressing me. Covered me with his body, his weight pressing me into the carpet, then entered and held still until I came, and came again. Talked me through it as if I were a virgin. *Breathe now,* he kept saying. *Darling. You need to take a breath.*)

TWO

Invisible, relentless, the erosion of human imprint upon the planet. The old enemy Nature gnawing steadily away, wind and water and invasive plant. Wet emergence of frond and fern, moss and lichen, vine and privet; the fierce sprawl of kudzu, sun surfacing over the vine-draped woods with a decorous goodwill (we tell ourselves) so we forget to notice the gradual rise in temperatures. The humid air oppressive, eerily still. Yet every so often, at twilight, a hot breeze, like a belly breath held and pushed suddenly outward, will arrow up the street, shuddering leaves in its path and bending tips of cattails newly sprouted from the ditch. One can almost see this breath from above: a single, fingerlike strand of air making its way toward the two-story house with its globed gas lamp flickering beside the dollhouse mailbox. It agitates the pine needles clogging the gutters of old Mrs. Lawson's house (Lady, her golden retriever, barking on the front porch—what does she sense this evening, as the wind ruffles her fur and she whimpers, then paws at the door to be let in?), stipples the surface of a swimming pool, and imperceptibly sways a faux hitching-post ring held forth by a statue of a black man in uniform. It cuts a path through the pokeweed and onion grass in the empty lot two doors down and winds through the grove of mulberry trees still dropping ripe fruit. It rushes past the row of crape myrtles next door, causing tiny pink petals to loosen and sink, silently, to the ground.

See it pause before the house on its swell of land, lower half lit, upstairs dark. (The daughter, wearing a thin white nightshirt, has flung off covers and sleeps on her stomach, the fine bones of her spine articulate in the dim nightlight, while across the hall, beneath a blanket printed with elephants, the son lies faceup, arms flung out, each soft palm curled as if cradling a cookie.) The air climbs up the front lawn and bends around the home's exterior geometries, shivering against window-panes. (The husband hears a rattle and looks up, briefly, to see his own pale reflection; he's working late, a client site in Chattanooga he will visit tomorrow, third-generation family-owned company desperate to hire women and minorities.) The air twists itself around the crabapple tree and crawls over the herb garden's sprawling mint and basil gone to flower. At the back of the house it presses against a window flickering with a faint blue light. (The wife is propped on pillows, reading light clamped to her book. She hears a gentle *tap* on the windowpane and reminds herself to cut back the butterfly bush. On the edge of sleep she feels an exhale on the back of her neck. Thomas? she says, reaching over to his vacant side of the bed.)

I think I'm going to write to him, Maggie says.

A Saturday morning in August. She and Thomas are sitting on the back porch. The children—teenagers—are both still asleep.

Who? Thomas says, raising his eyes from his laptop. His feet rest on the tempered glass coffee table between them. Magnolia leaves and pine needles litter the driveway, a storm that blew up overnight. The morning is cool, breezy, the crape myrtles glinting with raindrops. By noon it will be muggy again.

Maggie holds up a book. Always a book in her hand, in her purse, beside the bed.

James Abbott, she says. He's a formalist. Writes in a hyper-regular iambic meter, but with all this, I don't know . . . *riot* inside the lines.

Thomas nods. He's always been a good listener.

On the surface he's writing about the apocalyptic suffering created by a market economy, she says. He was part of the Occupy movement.

The Occupiers, Thomas says. Raising their Starbucks in collective protest.

He reminds me a little of Hopkins, she says, ignoring the slight. Recalibrating the language of faith. Assimilating the old ways of speaking about God and moving beyond them.

Read me something, Thomas says.

She knows this is his way when he feels threatened, to engage with her in the dialogue, attempt to understand what she's saying and entice her to go deeper. And in return for this openness—though she wouldn't call it that, something *in return,* it's just their way, a tacit agreement of sorts—she tells him everything. Usually more than he needs to know. That she would write to this poet, for instance.

She opens to her favorite poem, reads a few stanzas, looks up.

My God, Thomas says. You're gorgeous when you read, you know that?

From: Margaret Ellmann <magselm@gmail.com>
Date: August 12, 2013, 11:48 AM
To: James K. Abbott <jlabbott@princeton.edu>
Subject: hello & thanks

Dear Mr. Abbott:

I'm writing to tell you how much I admire your
new collection. I read it on a long flight. It was as
if I took off in one universe and landed in another.
The poetry unlocked something for me. Cleansed
my perception, somehow. Not sure how to describe
the experience. A renewed sense of holiness about
the world. It bolstered me in some crucial ways
regarding my own articulation of faith. On a panel
in Boston, with two male writers—both of whom
declared their own disdain for organized religion—
the moderator asked me, point blank, if I was a
believer. I'm not sure I would have answered in the
way I did, had I not been reading your book.

    I'm now making my way through the essays in
your *HABIT OF PERFECTION*.

    I've never written to an author I don't know
personally. But to quote C. S. Lewis, "A book
sometimes crosses one's path which is so like the
sound of one's native language in a strange country,
it feels almost uncivil not to wave some kind of flag
in answer."

I do hope I'll have the chance to meet you at some point. For now, my deepest thanks for your beautiful work.

Yours,
Maggie Ellmann

From: James K. Abbott
Date: August 17, 2013, 9:12 AM
To: Margaret Ellmann
Subject: RE: hello & thanks

Dear Maggie,

Thank you for taking the time to say these things,
and for being a soul of solidarity in this scary time of
cheery nihilism. Nietzsche and Camus and Beckett—
all of that *meaningful* madness—seem positively
companionable compared to the bland insanity of
today. Once writers staked their beliefs to church
doors or screamed them out of the flames. Now
we whisper into microphones at panels. Why can't
we have one Grand Panel (and maybe one Grand
Inquisitor?) and be done with it?
     I wish I knew what you said to that moderator!
     And there's some stupid stuff in *HABIT*. Try
not to hold it against me. I want to write a new
Foreword to the book but I can't keep up with the
work I already have in front of me. I can't keep up
with anything these days. I'm quite sure that's the
way your life is as well, as I believe you have the
same number of children as I do. I googled; am eager
to read *your* book. Linked stories about Southerners
preparing for an immanent second coming sounds
delightfully, subversively weird.

I'm surprised you have time to go to the
bathroom much less write me an email. But I want
you to know how grateful I am to you for waving
this flag. I hope to find a way to get you up to
Princeton, at some point, so we can sit and talk.

Yours, James
P.S. (*Mister Abbott?*)

Dear James (*James!*):

Yes, yes, the collective whisper from the dais. And
I plead guilty. I was writing a piece freelance, called
"The Christian Writer in Post-Christian America,"
a la Catholic Novelist in the Protestant South. I'd
written an entire section on my sense of isolation;
my grief, the longing for return to a viable literature
of faith. I pulled it just before the deadline. I
chickened out. I think it was the right thing to do.
The essay was soapboxy, and included a manifesto
against the "Christian publishing industry,"
which—I'll say it to you—has all but decimated real
theological understanding and continues to further
the demise of intellectual thought and discussion
re: religion in our country. I mean, what T. S. Eliot
feared might happen, in 1935, has happened. I'm
sure you know this quote but I'll paste it anyhow:
"The last thing I would wish for would be the
existence of two literatures, one for Christian
consumption and the other for the pagan world . . .
The greater part of our reading matter is coming
to be written by people who not only have no such
belief, but are even ignorant of the fact that there are
still people in the world so 'backward' or 'eccentric'
as to continue to believe."

As a matter of fact, my husband and I lived
in Princeton for several years. I was getting my
doctorate in comparative literature. Thank God

I didn't finish, I'm much happier on the creative side. Pregnancy and a move to Nashville, where we still live. I started another doctoral program, at Vanderbilt this time, the intersection of poetry and theology. And of course got sidetracked by eschatology, and wrote the strange little collection instead of finishing the dissertation. It seems a PhD is *not* part of the plan.

What I really wish I could do is write poetry.

We'd welcome an excuse to visit. Is Teresa Caffe still in Palmer Square? Our favorite Italian. And Chez Alice (those croissants!)?

Yours,
Maggie

Dear Maggie,

So you've studied here—all the more reason to
get you back. My wife and I will treat you to
dinner at Teresa, still here, yes, and our favorite
as well. If all else fails, I've just been invited to
give a lecture and teach a one-day workshop
during a conference in Nashville next summer.
Normally I decline such invitations—I find
conferences distracting from the real work, and
one comes away with a warped perception of one's
importance. But there's something in the timing
of the invitation, don't you think? Perhaps we're
fated to meet.

   In the meantime, let's keep talking. Have you
read Fanny Howe's *Indivisible*? I think you'd love it.
May I send you a copy? Give me your address and
I'll put it in the mail.

Yours,
JA

Dear James,

No, I haven't read it, and yes, I'd love a copy.
Address below.

I was invited to the same conference. Local girl
makes it big, haha. Never mind that almost no one I
know has actually read the book.

I will look forward to seeing you there, if not
sooner.

Yrs, ME

Dear ME:

Ah, the casual self-deprecation in your initials sign-
off. Me. Brilliant.

Here's the book. Write when you're finished. I'll
be curious to know what you make of McCool in
that closet.

Yrs, JA

p.s. —forgive my handwriting, I've never been
good at The Pen. I suspect it's why I became a
poet; one traffics in single words. I do feel an
immense gratitude for being born into the Era of the
Handheld Writing Utensil. Had I been born into the
keyboard generation I might have ended up—the
horror—a novelist.

Winters settle over the neighborhood, wet cloudy mornings, bright frigid afternoons, sometimes enough snow to get out the disc sleds and toboggans and head to the golf course, where families gather at the top of a steep hill. Hoots and hollers, frozen toes, tears, wet scarves, lost mittens. Fathers coast down with bright-cheeked toddlers nestled between their legs. Mothers with carafes of hot chocolate and tins of marshmallows huddle near cars, discussing travel plans and Christmas gifts.

Cooped up in the house, the dog compulsively rubs his muzzle along the front of the couch cushions. The son, dressed for a class Christmas party, slides down the banister. A balustrade snaps, the rail gives way, and he falls, fracturing his wrist. The husband drives the old gray cat to the vet twice a week for IV fluids, a low growl coming from the carrier in the backseat. Hey, Mr. Smokes, hey, old boy, hang in there. You've been a good cat, a good faithful cat. You've redeemed your species. You are so much better than I ever could have imagined you'd be, the husband says into the windshield, dragging his shirt cuff across his eyes.

A crack appears in the drywall where heights are marked in pencil, crayon, and marker—an ill-chosen spot, southern-exposed, the lower marks already disappearing. Wedgwood plates lined on a kitchen shelf grow furred with dust. A leaky dishwasher swells the underpinnings of the wood floor, until one morning a single plank heaves up and the daughter stubs a toe rinsing her cereal bowl. The hinges on the swinging door between the kitchen and dining room loosen. One day, when the dog crosses the threshold, the door swings suddenly shut on his tail. The dog yelps and instantly soils himself.

Down in the basement mildew eats into a jogging stroller's fabric, dark spots beginning to coalesce and multiply, until the great silent rending as a section of fabric slips from the frame and dangles wildly, for a moment, into open space.

Days grow warmer. The sledders at the golf course disappear. In the watery light of spring one hears only the *whish* and *ping* of drivers off tees, the whir of golf carts, the gentle *pock* of putters on clipped greens, flags snapping at the tips of their poles.

From: Margaret Ellmann
Date: July 21, 2014, 10:16 AM
To: James K. Abbott
Subject: poems attached

Dear James:

It was so great to meet you, finally, and spend time
with you here in Nashville. Thanks for making a day
of it with me.
    As promised, a poem. Two of them, in fact.
Caveat: they're bad. I'm a beginner. You must
picture me at your feet, an apprentice eager to learn.

Yrs, ME

The Withholding

Time for goodbye, father said.
I thought my uncle would say it,
but he said, No—we are the ones.

Beside a slatted blind, his arm lifted
and lifted from the wrist as if drawn
by a string. Father slid to the linoleum,

back to the wall. When he asked,
Why's he doing that?
he was his baby brother.

Reaching, the nurse said, for his
loved ones waiting.

I tried to feed him a sip of water.
He clamped the cut straw between
his teeth, where it stuck out—
rakish, like a cigar.

The nurse squeezed his cheeks
until the straw tumbled onto his
sheeted chest. Only if they ask, she said.

In the family lounge, I didn't weep
because I would miss him.
It was the water, that straw.
The fierce mercy of withholding.

Protestant Worshipper in Catedral Nogales,
Sonora, Mexico

Veronica is lovely. She wipes the dust from Christ's
    face in the carving
beside Simon, though she is never mentioned in the
    Gospels.

I watch a woman bald with cancer glue tiny silk
    roses to the hands, feet,
and side of the body hanging on the crucifix.
    Healing is the end

of all things. Inside the cathedral, the congregants
    wear collared shirts
and panty hose. Tomorrow they will sweep floors,
    pick cabbage.

We are no strangers to ritual. Some of us descend
    into rivers, enact death,
burial, and resurrection, a little embarrassed by our
    wet hair.

From: James K. Abbott
Date: July 21, 2104, 4:21 PM
To: Margaret Ellmann
Subject: RE: poems attached

Dear Maggie:

These poems aren't bad. Not by a long shot. The
first is quite stunning, the payoff of the final line,
which lands just right. Yeats's box clicking shut.

The second one is also good. I've done a bit of
tweaking. See what you think.

I think often and fondly of our day in Nashville.
Can we figure out a way to have a redux?

Yrs, JA

Dear James,

I feel like a caricature artist showing her sketches
to da Vinci! But I like your tweaks. Thank you for
taking time with these. For taking them seriously.
They're straightforward but that's probably the
only kind of "poetry" I'll ever be able to manage.
Who was it that said everyone wants to be a poet?
And when they fail they try to write stories; and,
failing at that, they give up and write a novel . . .
Faulkner? Updike?

   We do need a redux. I'd love to meet Beth. If
only we lived closer.

   I've been reading Lewis's sermons in *The
Weight of Glory.* The one on transposition—do
you know it? This idea that the language of faith
is a translation from a higher system to a lower.
Pepys wrote in his diary that when he was sick with
aesthetic pleasure, it was the same way he felt when
he was amorous with his wife, or sick with the flu.
In other words, the emotions were vastly different
but their biological manifestations were identical.
Of course the physical system is . . . clunkier, I
suppose. Less complex than the emotional. So the
lower system (physical) has to rely on the same
mechanisms to express the complexities of the
higher (emotion, psychology). Same with playing a
piece written for orchestra on the piano: the keys
must stand for flutes, violins, cellos, etc.

And so with the language of the sacred texts. Is it
any wonder, Lewis writes, that the Bible can furnish
nothing better for an Apocalypse than jewels, music,
crowns and thrones—the same old stuff from our
terrestrial existence? You see this in the mystics, too,
especially the medieval women visionaries. Erotic
language employed in the service of a love that's
far from sexual. Hadewijch, Beatrijs of Nazareth,
Mechthild of Magdeburg. Angela of Foligno
especially (her vision of love coming toward her as
a penetrating sickle!) The point is that we inhabit
the lower order, so when the higher tries to get in it
can only be transposition. But to dismiss the higher
order because the images seem childish would be to
refuse to look at a painting because it uses only two
dimensions. We wouldn't think of it. We understand
the translation.

I might write something about this. Maybe that
post-Christian-America essay after all.

It's nice, writing to you like this. I don't know
if I told you, when we were in Nashville, that
Thomas doesn't really go in for anything religious?
He's totally supportive. But talking about God with
someone who takes it seriously—well, it's something
I didn't know I was missing and now that it's
happening I realize how absolutely starved I was.

Yrs, ME

p.s.: I finally finished the Howe. McCool locked in that closet! Of course one thinks of every repression metaphor. But the way his imprisonment cages *her* is what's heartbreaking. She hasn't accomplished a thing, locking him in there.

Dear Maggie,

Da Vinci could have used some pointers from a
caricature artist!

I love that sermon, "Transposition." He gave it
on Pentecost. One of his best. That, and "Is Theology
Poetry?" I'm guessing you've got that one memorized.
He's right—evolution is the more poetic idea, the
fragile cell struggling upward, across millions of
years against impossible odds and the certainty of
extinction when the sun burns out. Tragic.

Yes, the medieval women visionaries. What
I've always found fascinating in Mechthild of
Magdeburg (now there's a throatful) is her desire
for an erotic relationship with *both* Christ and the
Virgin. Her intuitive understanding that spiritual
longing transcends binary concepts of masculine
and feminine. And how she gives Christ dual
gender roles: mother, sustainer, from whom she
wishes to drink blood (so much blood in these
visions) but also as one to whom she's eager to
submit, and from whom she wants to . . . well.
Receive his potency, so to speak.

As for getting together with Beth. She's warm
and wonderful and smart. But she's funny about
meeting my writer friends. She'd rather I talk
shop when she's not around. Now, if we could
talk landscape architecture . . . Did I tell you she's

designing a park for the blind? First one of its kind
in the state. Braille on the undersides of handrails,
along the edges of slides, on the chains of swings.
Flowers selected for scent signatures.

I've been listening—obsessively listening—
to Bach's English and French Suites. It's doing
something for me, metrically. I mean for my work.
Watch the attached clip, Glenn Gould playing a
gigue I love. (You know about his custom chair?)

Happy to chat about the poems on the phone,
if you'd like. A live voice is much superior to
this polished digital medium. Even handwritten
letters would be better. I miss the cross-outs, the
undisguised mess of rehearsal. Email is convenient
but one gets (and gives) something akin to a
performance.

Yrs, JA

p.s.: send more poems?

Parent meetings, medical forms, class photos, permission slips. Organelles. Passive versus active transport. Plant cell, animal, hypo, hyper, exo, endo. Periodic table. (A man behind iron bars gets out of prison, the son says, and when he's outside the gate, he goes, Finally, I'm fee. Iron, FE. It's a mnemonic.) Let me not to the marriage of true minds a rose by any other name if we spirits have offended out out brief candle. A-squared plus B-squared sine cosine line plane slope distance formula. Je suis tu es il/elle est nous sommes vous êtes ils/elles sont censure guile parsimony recalcitrant diffidence prosaic gravity electromagnetic strong nuclear weak nuclear Higgs boson dark matter multiverse theory wavefunction collapse Polyphemus Odysseus George Lennie Daisy Tom Gatsby Atticus Scout Huck Jim Hester Prynne Ralph Simon Jack Piggy Ministry of Truth Manor Farm World State Savage Reservation Big Brother is watching you're all a bunch of phonies. When in the course of human events we the people in order to form a more perfect four score and seven years 1492 1517 1776 1865 1914-18 1929 1939-45 1969 1989 1991 2001. Hitler Mussolini Churchill Warsaw. Dachau. Auschwitz.

The daughter studies, draws, practices the piano; she sings, warming up her voice to the highest notes. Ring-ee-*yah*, ah ah ah ah. Her friend calls the mother, after their senior class trip to the Holocaust Museum in D.C. I have to tell you something, Mrs. Ellmann, she says. You know how Kate wears all those bracelets? You should look underneath. I don't know why I do it, Mom, Kate says. I just feel sad and guilty all the time. Like I should be doing more. Or less. I don't know. Pediatrician, nutrition specialist, therapist. She seems to think a 4.0 is the expectation, Dr. Pierson says, the bare minimum. They finally give in to medication and within a month the daughter is happy again. Why'd we wait so long? Maggie says, her head on Thomas's chest. Are we terrible parents? I guess you learn along the way, Thomas says.

SATs, ACTs, college tours, early action, early decision, demonstrated interest, interviews. Tell us one thing you've done that's had *national impact*. Tears. A sunny fall day in Boston, crisp. On the tour the daughter buys a sweatshirt in the bookstore and wears it all weekend. They walk the Freedom Trail to the Italian district, passing impromptu bands, people in Halloween costumes handing out candy. The daughter is flushed and beaming, eating her calzone. I absolutely love it here, she says.

From: Margaret Ellmann
Date: July 23, 2014, 9:17 AM
To: James K. Abbott
Subject: RE: poems attached

Dear James,

Totally understand re: Beth. I would never want to
impose. Her park sounds fantastic, and important.
Thomas, too, can be a bit protective, or threatened.
Those aren't the right words. He's brilliant and
respected in his field. Right now he's helping a
company develop a ten-year IPO and merger and
acquisition plan. Or something like that. I wish I
could tell you more about his work, but I find the
language of business inaccessible.

I play that gigue. Years of piano lessons, still
with me. It's a lovely little piece. The lightness of the
voice on top twining with the heavy anchor of the
left hand—and then the way the voices trade places,
the layering creating a kind of third voice. And the
gorgeous fusion in the final chord.

Gould's a genius. My parents saw him live once
and walked out. It was awful, my mother said, the
way he kept buzzing and humming, how could
anyone stand it?

She had no idea who they'd walked out on!

A couple more attached. Help.

Yrs, ME

Foreknowledge

A man outside a bookstore
The tattooed wrist

Draws her toward him
Down into him

As into the pinions of a wing
All those years sealed

The wax
His mouth would break

She looks away
They know how it will be

She lies down
He tells her to lie down

Prayer

I asked to be where no storms blew.
Silence. So I asked for only a little rain,
Some wind, lightning, maybe thunder,
Hail even, but nothing more.

I said, At least you owe me this.
Rooftops blown off the city, felled
wires, blacked-out blocks, swath-cut
fields, tossed-over trailers, trees uprooted
like breech births. The city, fucked—

my house still standing,
the only one still standing.

In late July they drive to Lake Rabun, in the North Georgia Mountains. One of their last family trips before Kate leaves for college. A friend from work has given Thomas the keys to his custom lake house: three stories, exterior walls of glass facing the lake, a two-slip boathouse with a sundeck on its roof. The main entrance is on the third floor, a kitchen and living area furnished minimally, natural hardwoods, white linens, stainless steel. This place is *sick,* Tommy says. He strips to his boxers, runs down the steep staircase to the boathouse, and stands on the deck railing, whooping before plugging his nose and jumping off.

Thomas grins at Maggie and Kate, peels off his shirt, and does the same.

Kate watches them from the living room windows. I think these open, she says. Together, she and Maggie fold the doors into pleats, until there's nothing between them and the lake but a narrow balcony and a thin row of pine trees. The water glints jade in the noon sunlight. They change into swimsuits and walk down to the sundeck. The boys have already pulled out the stand-up paddleboards and are jousting, each trying to knock the other off. Kate looks over the edge of the rail.

How far a drop is it? she asks Maggie.

Twenty-five feet, maybe? Maggie says.

Well, I'm getting in like a normal person, Kate says, walking down to the dock and using the ladder. Thomas and Tommy fling water at her with their oars. *Stop,* it's *freezing!* she cries, slipping underwater. From above, Maggie watches the muscles in Thomas's back flare as he paddles up to Kate and jumps off his board, helping her climb on. He looks up.

Fifty bucks and dishes for a week if you jump, he calls.

Do it, Mom, jump! Tommy and Kate cry. Their slicked-back hair, the familiar shapes of their skulls—always she is startled, seeing them after a swim, or just out of the shower, by the layering of the past in their faces: baby, toddler, and child in palimpsest beneath the teenagers.

Not a chance, she says. I'll get us lunch.

In the kitchen she makes sandwiches. Turkey, heirloom tomatoes, avocado, Havarti cheese. She licks Dijon from her fingers. Sun on the water, depth of green in the trees on the opposite shore, laughter breaking the silence like shattered bits of glass—behind the peace of this moment is a new happiness. Whenever she thinks of it—of him—her present surroundings electrify.

At dusk they take the boat out for a ride up and down the lake's narrow channels. They pull into a small cove and drift. Thomas has brought his fishing gear. I'll bet there's some great bass in here, he says. And bluegill. Your favorite, remember, Katie?

I thought it was blue *girls* till I was probably fourteen, Kate says. I was always bummed they never turned out to be blue.

Maggie remembers the stocked pond at the golf course—the children seven and five, crouched together at the water's edge, a fish flopping between them in the grass. Thomas showed Kate how to lower the fish into the water and move it back and forth a few times, to circulate oxygen through the gills. *You don't want to throw him in, Katie bug, he'll get confused. You have to help him remember where he lives.*

You want to give it a try? Thomas asks now, holding out the pole to Kate.

Sure, Kate says. But if I catch one, you're taking it off the hook.

Hey, guys—say, *Blue Girl,* Tommy says, holding up his phone.

Potholes appear in the driveway. Flagstone pavers on the back patio flake off around their edges, leaving exposed patches of dirt where weed and moss appear. Invasive plants encroach, privet and wisteria, thistle and honeysuckle. The backyard steadily shrinks. The latch hook falls off the gate to the chicken run and a possum squeezes through, climbing the plank and entering the nesting box. The following morning the wife finds one of her hens dead, another still alive but with its crop ripped open. The rest are huddled on the roost. She removes the dead chicken from the coop and wraps the injured one in a beach towel, holding it steady against the grass while the son, stoic and wincing, stretches out the neck, one hand covering the eyes. The husband uses garden shears to cut the head off. I'm so sorry, he repeats, until the body beneath the towel yields to stillness.

From: James K. Abbott
Date: July 23, 2014, 9:56 AM
To: Margaret Ellman
Subject: RE: poems attached

Dear Maggie,

I didn't know you played! Next time we see one
another—whenever that might be—maybe you
could play that piece for me. We have a little
upright, a Yamaha. Caroline took lessons for a
while but it didn't stick.

The poems. I insist we speak about them
real-time. I can hardly remember what your voice
sounds like.

Do you read much apophatic literature? I'm
thinking of *The Cloud of Unknowing*. I'm deeply
interested in poetry or music—any art form—that
finds, or tries to find, God in this negative way. I
mean by describing what God isn't. The Western
cataphatic modes don't appeal to me anymore.

Sorry, rushing out, we're taking Caro dorm
shopping (!)

Yours, in haste,
JA

p.s.: let's not talk about our spouses?

From: Margaret Ellmann
Date: July 25, 2014, 3:25 PM
To: James K. Abbott
Subject: RE: poems attached

Dear James:

I'll do better: mp3 of me playing the Bach attached.
But I'm a bit terrified to speak to you on the phone,
about the poems. Maybe I don't want to hear what
you have to say!

   I read a good deal of Western apophatic
theology in grad school, but I've forgotten much of
it. Somehow it doesn't stick in the brain. Well, the
Summa Theologica, of course. (I had a great Aquinas
professor.) Also Meister Eckhart, and yes, *The Cloud
of Unknowing.* I do remember I came away with
the idea that what distinguishes Eastern mysticism
from Western is the concept of the self. I mean, in
Buddhism the existence of the self—the *illusion* of
the self—is a source of suffering. But in Christianity
it's not *that* I exist, but that I exist in separation
from God. We long for a perfect, noncontingent
existence, not for the annihilation of existence
altogether. Resurrection versus Nirvana. We see this
in the natural order, in human relationships. Far
from losing myself in . . . well, say in you, in these
talks, I feel I'm discovering, or recovering, a deeper
self, something at the core of my being. If it's true of

human relationships, why not of something beyond
humanity? Of course, this line of thinking wouldn't
hold a drop of water for an atheist.

We're college shopping here, too. Never thought
I'd spend so much money on goose down.

Agree about our spouses.

Yrs, ME

They stop going to church, except on holidays. Sundays the only chance to sleep in. The husband and wife pass one another in hallways, weary of trying to keep everything up. They live in the house helplessly, as if they're invalids. The son makes them laugh, shows them clips on his phone at dinner, people falling, failing. Walls are clustered with drawings, paintings, maps, photographs. One evening the husband stands on the landing of the staircase, looking at the artwork reaching almost to the ceiling. The wife pauses beside him. No one ever hung anything I made, he says. It's beautiful, what you've done for our kids. I don't say thank you often enough.

The gathered years: grains of spilled salt brushed from a table into an open palm. Each a nothing, barely noticeable—yet if you were to examine a single grain beneath a microscope, you would see a bright expanding flare: the daughter's agony over a college breakup, her stunned silence in the car on the way home from the airport, formal dance photos embossed with Greek letters shoved into a corner of her closet shelf. You would witness the son's outbursts of anger about limits placed on his video game time, his computer time. He throws his calculus textbook against the wall and it makes a parallelogram-shaped hole. He hangs a Japanese manga poster to hide it and the hole won't be discovered until he leaves for college. Hidden in the back of a drawer in the son's desk is a one-hitter a friend showed him how to make out of a fat highlighter pen, the buds stored in a baggie inside an old VHS cassette. A tiny red Bible sits on his nightstand, piece of gum folded into the downturned corner of a psalm.

From: James K. Abbott
Date: July 29, 2014, 6:12 AM
To: Margaret Ellmann
Subject: RE: poems attached

Dear Maggie:

Thank you for the music. Beautiful. The fact that
you can just sit down and play like that. I envy you
that talent.

It is indeed humanity's Great Failure, that we go
on trying to exist apart from God . . .

Listen, I hardly meet anyone, anymore, who
thinks this way. You were raised evangelical?
I can hardly believe it. You seem—how to put
this—open to ways of thinking that move beyond
personal ethics. Our collective moral collapse
far exceeds the personal. Evangelicals go around
saying Christianity's about a personal relationship
with Jesus, but they don't talk about rebuilding the
ruins of the world, about getting politically active.
An entire continent dying of AIDS, massacre in
Syria and Sudan, reefs dying, global temperatures
soaring—and most right-wing Americans are
hunkered down trying not to commit any gross
moral failings.

Tell me more about your kids. Do they use
Snapchat as their primary means of communication,
as mine do? And your family, growing up. Siblings?

Pets? Paint me the full picture of Little Girl Maggie.
I want to know the child who became the naked
mind I hope to find in my in-box every day. It's a
mind I'd like to keep close. For a lifetime, if possible.

Yours—Yours.

From: Margaret Ellmann
Date: July 29, 2014, 12:10 PM
To: James K. Abbott
Subject: RE: poems attached

Dear James:

Yes, this Snapchat thing—Tommy loves it. I've got the app but I don't know how to use it. I'll probably have to learn, if I want to stay in touch with him once he leaves for college. He wants to apply to NYU and Columbia, by the way. We were hoping he'd check out schools in Boston but he's got his heart set on New York. Funny, we started out up there and moved down here and now the kids are migrating back. If he winds up in the city, maybe we could figure out a way to see one another. I'd love to have coffee, or lunch.

And I don't need to tell you, what it was like to grow up in the desert! Though I imagine Phoenix and Santa Fe had very different flavors . . .

Do you want to talk live? Do you ever Skype? I'm home if you want to. Magselm72.

Yours, yours, too.

It's the summer that destroys. The hot exhaled breath. Like the Angel of Death in the old cartoon the children used to watch. It gathers force. It knocks over an Adirondack chair and shoves together the long bamboo wind chimes strung from a branch, leaving in its wake a hollow *Ohhh*. At sunset the old black Lab barks hoarsely at the bright plate of moon above a lit cloud, a storm system that will erupt overnight. His ears draw back, he sniffs the air and blinks, as if listening.

THREE

Attempt to go back and locate her earliest sexual yearnings. Suspicion that an explanation for Chicago—if there is an explanation—lies in the past. A recurring dream, when she was ten or eleven: a dusty Sunday school classroom at the back of a church. She was alone, lying on a cot, looking up at a high window cut into adobe brick. Typical desert construction, windows sized long and rectangular to let in light but keep out heat. A slurred sunlight came through the window—red-orange, just-rising or just-setting—while somewhere far off, on a tinny piano, someone played "The House of the Rising Sun." A death song, she thought when she woke. A song they might play at a funeral, possibly hers. She was on the cot—though sometimes, in the dream, she was slung into a wheelchair—her legs were spread, she was unable to move while the old light shifted down the wall and along the floor toward her; a deep pleasure in the paralysis, the inability to fight off the color now sliding up her thighs.

Go back further. Outcomes, Maggie thinks, lie in the exigencies of the past. The fifth-grade friend, Karen, who showed off her new bra, then told Maggie to lift up her own shirt so she could see Maggie's chest. Anika, in third grade, the way her fingers felt when they played hospital, giving Maggie a shot, or wrapping her broken leg in toilet paper—the way Anika's touch made Maggie's lower stomach quiver.

Maybe all desire begins this way, she thinks. With friends, moving outward.

Further back. Cleveland, 1955. Her father and his brother, the rich uncle, eight and ten years old. They take turns playing the piano all afternoon and evening while their mother, her grandmother, keeps time with a pencil. *Tap tap tap, tap tap tap.* On the top floor, *her* mother—their grandmother, Maggie's great-grandmother—is dying. She wants to hear the piano, the sound of young fingers on keys drifting up the steep carpeted staircase and down the hallway into the dim room with the giant four-poster bed and dusty afternoon light. The boys play Bach. When they tire, one boy does the left hand, one the right, trying to match tone for tone, until the grandmother calls down *Irish love songs a sonata a nocturne for God's sake play something else* so one digs for music while the other tries to play by ear, as loudly as possible, not for the grandmother's sake but to drown out the guttural sounds she makes when her medicine begins to wear off. Their wrists aching, fingers growing stiff into the night—the price her father paid to grow up in that house, to finally leave and get married to her mother and raise Maggie, paying for her piano lessons, sending her to UCLA and, eventually, out into the world so she could get married and have her own children and give them a happier, a more *stable* life than he had.

Every morning, her father once told her, I woke up hoping she'd died while I slept.

Bucket showers, Kate says at dinner. And the water's hot only if you're lucky. Americans have *no* idea.

January, 2017. Their daughter is just home from India, two weeks in a tiny village on the border of Nepal doing her field research project over the holiday break. She's an anthropology major, studying educational opportunities for young girls in the Tibetan refugee community. She has her hair twisted up in a scarf, wears a cropped T-shirt and balloon-shaped pants printed with lotus flowers. She's barefoot, her toenails painted light green. Thin, Maggie thinks, but she looks healthy. They're having dinner, stew and bread. Candles and wine, to welcome her home. Thomas has lit the fire in the dining room. Wiggins lies beside him, next to the hearth. Every so often he lifts his head and licks Thomas's hand, hoping for a bit of bread. Lately he's been dragging his back legs. Maggie keeps examining his paws for cuts, thorns, bruises, but can find nothing.

It's an amazing country, Kate says. All the color, and the just, I don't know. *Life.* I saw a monkey riding on a pig with a bird sitting on the monkey's head. Puppies everywhere. In Varanasi, on this one street—well we'd call it an alley—I got trapped between a cart of cow dung and a dead body. It was wrapped up in orange but a foot was sticking out, right next to my face. Hindus want to die there, if you die in Varanasi it's automatic *moksha.* Oh, and we took boats out on the Ganges to watch the Aarti priests at night, you float these candles and flower petals out and offer a prayer to the goddess. And Gangtok—Kanchenjunga is right there. Third highest in the world, you can't believe anything is that tall, it makes its own weather and when the wind blows the snow it looks like clouds. The air is clear, and the Tibetan people are so happy. I can't wait to go back.

Luminous, Maggie thinks. Radiant, at twenty-one, the years of fighting through anxiety melted away. Was it the medication, therapy, biofeedback exercises? How did she come out the other side?

She and Tommy are the reason for my existence, Maggie thinks. The reason all of this exists.

When love is present in a home, the children almost always emerge beautifully into adulthood, Dr. Pierson said to them at Kate's last session. It's been a pleasure working with her, he said, shaking their hands. And with both of you. Whatever you've been doing, keep doing it.

Mom, Kate says. Let's go this summer. I could get Deepak to pick us up in Delhi and then Tenzing could meet us in Siliguri. We could do a trek from Yuksom, it's this charming little village. There's even a nice hotel, with electricity.

I'd love to, Maggie says. I'll think about it. I have this trip to Chicago coming up.

I meant to tell you, Thomas says. That company in Chattanooga I've been working with—they're doing a corporate retreat in Turks and Caicos in April. Spouses are invited and the CEO wants us to come along. It's at *The Palms,* Mags. Scuba diving off a reef, private yacht . . .

I committed to Chicago a while ago, Maggie says. I thought you were going to come with me?

They really want me there, Thomas says. But you're right,

Chicago was first. Let's keep talking about it.

Damn, I'll go if Mom can't, Tommy says.

On his walk the next morning, Wiggins collapses at the bottom of their street, legs splayed. C'mon, you lazy boy, Tommy says, pulling the leash. Wiggins pants and swallows, over and over, saliva pooling on the concrete. Each exhale sounds like a roar.

Let's go, Wiggins, Tommy says. You can make it.

The dog lays his head on the pavement.

Tommy runs up the hill, gets the car, and drives back. Wiggins hasn't moved. He lifts him into the hatchback. You need more exercise, old buddy, you're out of shape. For a moment he puts his face against the wiry gray fur around his muzzle, letting Wiggins lick the stubble on his chin, the way he likes.

Laryngeal paralysis, the vet tells Maggie. There's a surgery to tack open the larynx, but the risk of aspiration pneumonia is high. Anyhow it's a neurological condition, progressive. There's an oral medication that seems to work in some dogs, for the short term.

The vet pauses.

Many owners decide to wait before they make the decision to euthanize, he says. Others make the decision right away, to prevent any needless suffering. It's a very personal choice.

But he's happy, Maggie says. He never stops wagging.

It's his breed, the vet says. I had a Lab in here last week that was hit by a car. Broken bones, fractured skull, sections of skin missing—he was still wagging when I put the IV in.

At dinner—Wiggins panting, upright and eager—they discuss the timing with Kate and Tommy. Both children are home from school for a few more days, able to say goodbye. Maggie notices Tommy's face is flushed, his eyes bloodshot. From crying or weed she can't tell. The mixture of boy and man, his expression attempting to locate itself somewhere in the middle, fragility and stoicism shifting across his face.

It's not fair to let him suffer, Thomas says.

Can't we do the surgery? Kate asks.

It's risky, and it wouldn't help for very long, Maggie says.

He's had an incredibly long life for his breed, Thomas says.

Pets are a fucking waste, Tommy says, chin quivering. They're just ticking time bombs of sadness.

Two days later, when Thomas comes home with the ashes—Wiggins's collar wrapped around the embossed container—Tommy stands up from the computer.

We should bury him, he says. I'll dig the hole.

June 6, 2018

Dear James,

I can't remember the last time I wrote to you. I've lost the old journal . . .

That's a lie. I threw it out. Where did I learn that the word *repentance,* in the Greek, connotes more than just admission of fault—that built into the word is the idea of a 180-degree turn, a deliberate facing away from the wrong? Throwing out the journal was my attempt to make such a turn. I regret it now. Regret it because I can't look back to see if I've made any progress, and because reading the old letters to you ignited in my body, again, the feelings only you have ever accessed—little aftershocks, nothing like the eruption but sometimes approaching it. Connection points that could, if I allowed them to, take me from *here* to *there.*

This journal's new, leather-bound, with a thin cord that wraps around the exterior. Kate brought it home from India last year. I put the journal away till now. I imagined I would send it to you with one of my prayer-letters written on the first page. I imagined you would write a letter on the next page, and send the journal back to me, and it would become our habit, back and forth over the years. No telephone or emails or texts. A kind of analog redemption, a quiet return— not the fire this time, but the embers, subdued and tepid. A warmth we could keep, and stir every so often, just enough to expose a subtle but still-pulsing glow.

The heat is unbearable this summer, the humidity oppressive. All we're doing is lying around inside, drinking from cans of flavored sparkling water. Today I sat on the back porch to read—do you know Jane Gardam's Old Filth trilogy? (Why do I ask questions in these letters to him, God? The way I used to ask things of you?)—and when I let the chickens out to roam they just stood there with their beaks open, stunned.

Kate's home, we went shopping. She's about to leave for Paris, where her boyfriend's starting grad school. I bought an off-the-shoulder shirt for Florida next week. 25 years.

Something's happened to my body, some turnover in my genes. A sudden all-over aging. I can't stand to look at myself in the mirror. Or look down at my hands when I type. The fingertips are puckering, on their undersides, the way they used to in the swimming pool. I catch myself making a point about something to Thomas—extending my hand out onto the table, palm up, my fingers pressed together, as if I'm pleading—and I lose my train of thought, looking at the puckers. My grandmother used this palm-up gesture. I wonder if I'm doing it in remembered imitation, or if it's something hardwired into my DNA. This is what I mean, this all-over aging has turned me into a younger version of my grandmother, as if I can see her body waiting beneath mine. The upper arms loosening, a ballooning midsection, no matter how many crunches I do; little age spots on my thighs and chest, the backs of my hands. I hate caring about these things, but I do, I understand the impulse to dye and inject, plump certain places and shrink others.

Look around you, Mags, Thomas says. You're in better shape than 95 percent of the women your age.

But I remembered the night at dinner in Chicago—just before we left for the film—when you said you loved two things on a woman, wrinkles and gray hair. How beautiful, you said, a woman who's *earned* her face. I assumed you meant to be kind, noticing the silvering at my temples and how my crow's-feet had deepened since we last saw one another. Thomas means to compliment me. But his version still holds youth as the standard, whereas yours dispenses with the standard entirely.

She died last month, my grandmother. Increasing vertigo, a walker, oxygen, a wheelchair. Congestive heart failure. We all hoped she'd make it to a century. I wonder if yours is still living? Sometimes I imagine they might have died on the same day, and now, together, they're commiserating, or celebrating. Maybe talking about us.

I wish I would have told her about you. Nashville, New York, Chicago. All of it. I got this letter from her, after the funeral, enclosed with a set of handkerchiefs she'd embroidered. She wrote it the day after my wedding and didn't send it. Twenty-five years just sitting there with my name on it. My parents didn't even open it when they were going through the house. If we were still talking I would call and read you her letter. She would have understood us. It's a consolation, to know there was someone I might have told. *Grandma, I fell in love with another man.* Sometimes when the house is empty (always empty now, such an adjustment for the one who stayed home with the children, Thomas has no idea) I practice saying the words out loud. Different ways of saying it, depending on the listener. I committed adultery, I say to my mother. I fell in love with another man, I say to my best friend. We fucked, it meant nothing, I say to Thomas.

It was the best thing, I say to you. In all my life, the very best thing.

I imagine writing all this down and giving the manuscript to my agent.

This has been done to death, she says. I won't be able to sell this.

So you see: There is no one left to whom I can confess. No one who will listen or understand. There is you, and there is God. I'm not sure, anymore, there's a difference.

Chicago. April, 2017. A late dinner after the keynote speaker, nearly nine by the time we were seated, a group of us crowded around a long table beside the street-facing windows. Twelve writers and musicians, some with partners and spouses in tow. No one James or I knew. We were squeezed together in the middle of the table, our chairs facing the glass.

Outside the rain was beginning to taper off. Umbrellas, parkas, taxis hurrying past. Beneath the table I slipped out of my wet suede boots—there'd been no time to get back to the hotel to change.

Where in L.A.? the man beside James was saying.

I haven't found a place yet, James said.

You should check out Pasadena, I went to high school out there. Twenty years ago. Now there's train service to downtown, I mean public transportation is making L.A. almost *livable.*

Don't get me wrong, I love my students, but the quality of work just isn't the same, a woman at the far end of the table said. I recognized her, a writer who'd just come out with a novel reimagining F. Scott Fitzgerald as a sea captain.

Do you teach? the playwright on the other side of me asked. Beard down to his chest. He'd just ordered his third whiskey sour.

I'll have a visiting appointment next fall, I said. A small college between Nashville and Chattanooga.

Never teach unless starvation looms, he said.

Poets are lucky, the Fitzgerald woman said. No worries about agents or advances or royalties, I mean the *freedom . . .*

Poets have agents, the woman across from me said. You have one, right, James?

Well, it isn't the *norm*, the Fitzgerald woman said.

Let's go do something, I said to James, speaking low so no one else could hear.

Where?

There's got to be a movie theater nearby.

My flight's at nine tomorrow.

Mine's at eight. Nicholas Sparks, sci-fi. Anything.

I'll call a car, James said, putting cash on the table for our drinks.

We haven't even ordered yet! the Fitzgerald woman said, as we got up to leave.

The onset of darkness, in northern climates: get inside, get warm, light fires. And the desert's great reversal, year-round: twilight signals *egress*. The waning heat, the hour of going out, of something about to happen—every time she visits home in Phoenix, sunset urging her to drive somewhere fast, to embrace, be embraced—and it's that twilight excitement she feels in Chicago, in the museum, James looking at her in the mirror, the sweep of his gaze exposing, or creating, the dark truth of her situation: Her passion is dormant and something else altogether. A desire to be on her knees, to beg, then yield to pain. A wide-sky longing—what chance did she stand, when she met its counterpart?

When she has thrown up in the bathroom and cleaned her face and teeth and returned to the bedroom; when she has told James to fuck her again, when she is bent over the stacked pillows and he's wedged himself inside, not quite gently, a finger moving in front—when she's finally *there*, it's as if she's falling into herself and flying out of herself, both things at once, it is as close to the ecstatic as she has ever come, and knows she ever will come.

What he tells her to say is *Please.*

And, when she's finished: *Thank you.*

*Y*ou're going to have to probe the domination/submission aspect of this.

I have.

And?

Identification with Christ, who gave himself—voluntarily—unto death. Threw his arms wide and, in radical obedience to the Father, said, *I submit*. Dominance and submission part of the Divine nature.

Have you considered the similarity to the position that Thomas—

Or take Mary. Her submission to the Holy Spirit, brooding over her at the moment of conception. I am thy servant, may it be done unto me.

You're saying that you and James, in that moment, were a metaphor for . . .

That's the idea.

Yet I feel this absolves you of responsibility for what happened. You seem to want to portray yourself as a victim of your strong feelings, but I don't get the sense you have any agency about them. Even the way you speak of Thomas, the ways he's forced you—it's as if you believe you have no autonomy.

I admit to using my religious beliefs to manipulate, resisting temptation as a means of feeding my own desire.

I admit the fact I have had intercourse with only one man gives me a source of power. I admit to using it. In James's case, making sure he knew how untouched I was.

I admit to *playing up the innocence angle.*

I admit that I have created, to some degree, a self-feeding monster, using, at first, the emotional connection with James to further retreat from Thomas, creating an overall mien of frustration in our sex life. Sometimes I think I've given Thomas no choice but to continue to force himself on me, and I use this fact to subconsciously ("above all the heart is deceitful") justify both my feelings for James and my continued imaginative replaying of the night in Chicago. (The blue flame, James said at the airport. We'll extinguish the fire, we'll never speak again but we must keep the blue flame alive. Both of us. Promise me. I need to hear you say the words.)

I admit that my self-flagellation is indulgent and coercive. Guilt as fuel, guilt as food, guilt as energy.

I admit that I am not a victim but know what I want and how to get it by pretending, to myself, that I don't want it; maybe even lying to myself about my religious beliefs, because if I don't believe any of them the forbidden aspect of my sexual relationship with James will disappear, taking the pleasure with it.

I admit that if I do believe what I say—eternal forgiveness from before all time—the word *forbidden* becomes meaningless, everything becomes permissible. Why feel guilt for something preemptively forgiven? Why not simply acknowledge Chicago as planned, ordained—a cause, even, for celebration? (Grandmothers clink wineglasses in some crystal room dripping with jewels. All is well, they say. All shall be well and all shall be well and all manner of thing shall be well.)

I admit that unless something is forbidden I cannot want it with any intensity.

I admit that unless something is forbidden I can't *fucking feel anything.*

I admit that I loathe God for creating the universe in such a helpless situation—knowing it would get itself into this kind of trouble, creating it anyhow.

I admit that with Thomas I have autonomy. I am an adult. I could leave, for example. The children are grown. The house is empty.

I could simply leave.

(But would you leave a husband who, when you wake in the middle of the night, your body slick with sweat—dreaming you had to say goodbye to a man you slept with, once upon a time, but the man doesn't care, he has better things to do, he doesn't mind that he'll never see you again and the pain in your chest is so acute it forces you awake, gasping for air— this husband gets up to bring you a glass of water, then holds your hand across the mattress until you fall asleep? A man who, when your son brings home a girl who dropped out of high school and wants only to get married and have a kid, sits with her for an hour and talks about the benefits of higher education, offers to pay for her to take the GED and apply to colleges? Would you leave such a man? Or would you think: confess, repent, he is the one who should leave?)

January 9, 2017

Dear James:
Since we saw one another in New York I've been wondering
if I made the right decision, to no longer write, as it's been

Dear James:
Do you remember the moment we got to 24th just as the light
changed and I crossed while you waited

James:
I keep thinking about the churches, how if only we could
have gone inside one of them– if we'd spent time in a place of
worship, maybe prayed together—I mean I wonder if I might
have changed my mind

James: I know I insisted on this silence but I keep wanting
to discuss some of the poems in the Olds book you gave me,
"The Talkers," for instance, *it must be how the angels live,*
and how Milton felt the highest form of intercourse was
sexless, the intellectual interpenetration of angels. *My God,
they're not going to touch each other*—that line breaks my
heart every time

My friend how I've missed your voice since New York

My dear James

Dearest James

From: Margaret Ellmann
Date: January 10, 2017, 11:16 AM
To: James K. Abbott
Subject: Hello

Dear James:

Apologies for breaking the silence I so insisted on
in New York. Briefly: I wondered if you would be
at the conference in Chicago, in April? I'll be giving
a reading. I thought I should let you know. I'm
guessing you'll be there too. Thomas is planning to
come with me.

I hope you're well, and staying warm up there.

My Best,
Maggie

From: James K. Abbott
Date: January 10, 2017, 11:23 AM
To: Margaret Ellmann
Subject: RE: Hello

Dear Maggie,

How wonderful to see your name in my in-box!
No worries about breaking the silence. As you
know, I always thought maintaining a professional
conversation was the better route.

I'll be in Chicago, yes. Beth can't come. But I'll
look forward to meeting Thomas. (Finally!)

Cold, yes. Bring some of that southern warmth
with you?

Yours, JA

Dear James,

Thank you for this reply. I admit I was worried about breaking my own rule. You're right: better to simply leave the door open for professional communication.
　　Till Chicago, then. Looking forward.

Best, ME

Maggie:

Actually, might we speak on the phone? I have some
news I wanted to share before Chicago. Email too
impersonal.

Yrs JA

James,

Sure. Tommy and Kate are home until the end of next week. Can we talk the following week, say Monday, Jan 23?

Yours, ME

June 12, 2018. Twenty-five years. Her parents send them a cast aluminum sign, white, with embossed letters painted hunter green: ELLMANN, Est. 1993.

Kate's gone to Paris to visit her boyfriend. (*Maman,* she says, when she calls, *Mummy, you and Dad have* got *to get over here, we want to take you to the d'Orsay, you'll love it, and Père Lachaise, you can see Chopin's grave!*) Tommy home for the summer, working at a local organic farm. They leave him in charge of the house and go to Florida for a week, Naples, a high-rise hotel facing the sea. In between the hotel and beach is an estuary and a forest of mangroves. Golf carts shuttle guests back and forth along a wooden plank walkway. Maggie and Thomas prefer to walk. They have a suite on the eighteenth floor, where, in the living room, a double-wide chaise faces a floor-to-ceiling mirror. Assumption built into the arrangement of furniture.

You will enjoy it, Maggie tells herself. You will *give.*

His desire, and her fear, have become tempered, now. Blunt-edged, eroded. It's as if they've worn down together, and what's left is understanding and kindness. The quiet-spread-of-light kind of love, the placid excellence of long accomplishment. The flagstone patio, in the big house, the wearing away of sharp edges so only the central parts of the pavers remain; in the spaces between, dark soil sprouting the exploding weeds the children used to call firecrackers. And this is my husband, Maggie thinks. Softened around the edges, the essential part of him solid, the largest part of him only good. Better than I am. Maybe marriage is for this, she thinks. The shearing away of the rough, leaving the parts that will last into eternity.

Thomas unpacks and showers while she stands naked in front of the mirror. Her waist and hips are still defined, the skin just starting to loosen at the inner thighs and upper arms. Her calves and ankles will stay slim until she is ancient. Her grandmother's swollen ankles: what she remembers, remembering the last time she saw her. The hike of her pant legs when she sat, the quashy-thick skin inside nude compression stockings. She wonders about James's grandmother, in Santa Fe—if she's still living—and her belief in the Native ways, the continued presence of ancestors, how they would appear and speak to her. *My grandmother would love to talk about those visions you've been having,* James would write, if they were still writing.

Of every excuse to contact him, this seems the most natural. *Dear James, my grandmother died.* No one else she knows would understand what it meant to lose a grandparent at her age. To have watched one's children grow into adulthood with three generations behind them.

Long days on the beach, cushioned chairs set out for them each morning, striped towels, an oversized umbrella positioned to block the morning sun from behind. Young men in collared blue shirts come around to reposition the canopy, as the sun moves, seesawing the spiked post deep into the sand. Beside her Thomas is reading a galley of a book she's been asked to blurb. (Blurb? Thomas says. Like whatever happens to dribble out of your mouth?) They haven't fought in over a year. How ironic, she thinks, how inexcusable, that we've reached this peace now. She wonders if his patience with her began with what happened in Chicago—if somehow, in committing the act with James, she finally relaxed enough to free Thomas, and herself.

Only now I'm a slave to guilt, she thinks. To protecting a secret. She envisions the unconfessed truth growing like a malignant bead just beneath her skin, somewhere unnoticeable—armpit, inner ear. She's constantly scanning her body for strange moles, running soapy palms over her breasts in the shower. How many years must they live through before the fact of the affair no longer matters to him, or matters less? How long before she is safe? If she could say, "Five years ago, in Chicago, I did such and such"? Ten years? Fifteen?

She pictures her life as a time line on a blank page, progressing steadily upward, with three barely perceptible dips below the baseline as it approaches the center axis: MBA friend, minister, Aquinas professor. Minor temptations, really, looking back. Then a deep drop, right at the middle of life, a sharp downward spike pooling in a thick black mark at the bottom of the page. Chicago. From there the line begins to crawl upward, until a point in the future where it breaks the surface of the original baseline, never dropping below it again.

What is that point? When one of their children gets married? The birth of their first grandchild?

Mojitos, rum and cokes, pina coladas. The first drink energizes; the second numbs. By the third Maggie is in reverie, watching Thomas out in the water, floating on his back. The sea is waveless, flat to the horizon, the color of a gemstone in her best friend's ring. What was it called? Peridot. Afternoon Gulf is peridot. Peridot is Gulf afternoon.

A little girl calls from the water: *Grammy, watch us!* The grandmother on the next chaise over waves to two young girls with their father. She sits with her knees pulled up, wears a one-piece suit with shorts and a sun visor, her hair in a thin ponytail. In ten years I'll be her age, Maggie thinks.

The father is fit, tan, he lifts the girls over his head and throws them up and out, their bodies tucked into cannonballs. *Again!* they cry. The mother sits in a low chair placed at the water's edge. It is the grandmother they call to, she is the celebrity of the family.

The girls charge up the beach, scattering sand.

Grammy, the water's your temperature exactly!

Literally, Grammy!

Come swim with us!

Please!

In a little while, the grandmother says.

The girls run back to the water. *Watch this splash! Watch my dive!* The grandmother smiles, waves, it is enough for everyone.

Let me be the kind of grandmother who gets into the water, Maggie thinks.

In the opposite direction, toward the jetty, a teenage boy performs gainers for a group of girls in neon-bright bikinis. He runs forward and flings himself up and back, landing on his feet each time. A power move, a ninja move. The girls applaud, arching their backs, adjusting the ties on their swimsuits and tossing their hair. Maggie's own hair is a copper spill down her back, whiting only at the temples. Two months ago she noticed a few white hairs beneath her bikini bottoms and decided to wax everything away. How strange to see that part of her body hairless again, now, in middle age. Thomas loves the slick surface, the heightened lubrication. Since she's waxed he wants to kiss there all the time. She didn't think to wax, or even shave, in Chicago. The fact of their bodies—her own, James's—had seemed beside the point. As if mouths and tongues and limbs were only in the way, something they had to get through in order to get to something else.

A steady breeze ruffles the umbrella's border. From out in the water Thomas calls to her; she rises and walks to the edge, light-headed in the sudden sunlight, her limbs gritty with sand. She wades in, tiny fishes scatter, the water so warm she cannot feel it against her skin. Stepping into the sea it's as if she's entering negative space. Thomas stands where the shallows drop off, the line where peridot turns to slate. She wades out and slides into his arms. He holds her weightless, his hands beneath her thighs.

Hey, he says.

Hey. You've been out here a while.

I can't remember the last time I felt this relaxed.

I know, same.

You still in the wooden hat book?

Yeah. What did Kate say?

She wants to move, of course. She's talking about getting a work visa until she can apply to grad school.

And Tommy?

Everything's fine. It's hot, he got chigger bites from mountain biking on an uncleared trail. Listen, let's go back to the room. I have a present for you. Anyhow, look at the sky.

January 23, 2017

Hello?

Maggie?

Hey.

Good to hear your voice. It's been—what—six months?

Five I think. Since New York. How were your holidays?

Fine. Different this year . . .

I know, weird to have everyone under one roof again when you've gotten used to the quiet.

How's your work?

Good. I mean, slow, but good. What about you?

Great. Steady.

I saw the *New Yorker* poem.

That one isn't any good. Maggie—

You had news—

Beth and I are separating. Just a trial thing. With the kids gone . . .

That's—my God I'm sorry to . . .

. . . we don't have much to say to one another. We got married so young. I'm the one who's moving out.

I'm sorry—

I took a job in L.A. I'm moving out there at the end of the term.

What about Princeton?

It's a visiting appointment. UC Irvine. The plan is to come back. Beth and I don't really want to . . . I mean we hope it's not permanent. For now, with Dustin at Occidental—it'll be good to be close to him.

Right, he's in L.A. now.

You're the first person I've told outside of work.

Why me?

Because you're my friend.

Yes.

I'm looking forward to meeting Thomas in Chicago.

I was going to tell you, he's going to Turks and Caicos that week, for a company retreat. I might go with him.

Please don't.

All the spouses are going. Golf outings. Hors d'oeuvres on yachts. You'd love it.

I would understand if you went. But don't.

I haven't decided. I've heard you get blacklisted from the conference for three years if you cancel so I'm not—

Maggie. I lied. I haven't been able to write since we stopped talking.

. . .

Not a single, fucking poem. I feel like poetry is dead in me.

It's been the same for me.

Come to Chicago.

I'll think about it.

I want to say more.

Don't.

The rain comes. As it does every afternoon this time of year. Furious storms that end as abruptly as they begin. The massive buildup of cloud behind the high-rise condos and hotels along the shore, articulation of blue and green fading to gray. Families coalesce, gather belongings, and disappear; young men sweating through collared shirts pile umbrellas and chairs on the backs of four-wheelers. Shutters shut on beachfront bars, wind flaps the palms and grape plants with their exaggerated fruits, the first heavy raindrops pock the sand. An hour later it's over, the sun descending into the water, an orange-yellow flare at the horizon softening to the lavender of twilight.

Thomas and Maggie ride the golf cart back to the hotel. The wind is picking up; white birds flap over the mangrove forest; beneath the plank walkway, in the estuary, schools of tiny silver fish scatter across the surface of the water like flung rice. Yesterday, running on the beach, she'd seen a porpoise surfacing and diving, carving a scalloped line parallel to her own path. On the way back, crossing the bridge, she paused with a group of tourists taking pictures of a manatee in the estuary at low tide. Together they watched as it shapelessly rolled itself back to the sea.

From their room on the eighteenth floor Thomas and Maggie watch the storm, rain seeming to hover in midair like thick static, obscuring as if with smoke the high-rise condo building opposite, painted butter yellow with white-railed balconies stacked one above the other. The condo's parking lot is always empty, at night the windows are dark. (No one lives here in the summer, a couple they meet tells them. No one is *from* here either. It's a town you end up in.)

They're both naked, wet swimsuits in a heap on the floor. She lies back on the chaise in front of the mirror, watching herself touch her own breasts. Thomas above her, kissing everywhere. Two mojitos and a rum and coke in her system. She rolls her head to look outside, the sun already beginning to lighten the clouds. A sliding warmth against her skin. Lovely, to feel this again with a husband—

You taste like salt

You too

Your skin I still can't get over how soft

Why don't you—I want you

She is pulling him against her, arching up into him, lovely

Hold on, I want to get your present.

Thomas walks to the closet and comes back with a cloth drawstring bag.

Tell me that isn't what I think, she says.

It isn't. Not entirely.

She sits up. Inside the bag is a silver device, long and sleek.

Silver anniversary? he says.

Maggie stands, sets the device on the chaise, and begins to dress.

Come on, Mags, Thomas says. A little fun. And it isn't my only—

She pulls on her underwear, shorts, a tunic.

This is about that poet, isn't it, he says. The one you used to write to.

Everything tilting sideways. Where were her shoes?

This is about me, she says, grabbing a room key and—still barefoot—walking out.

On a lobby phone she dials James's cell number. Hangs up.

Dials again, lets it ring twice. Hangs up again.

She goes outside. Marble staircases, thatched-roof bar, pools, waterfalls. A children's waterslide obscured by palms and jungle flowers in violent bloom. The storm has let up, birds are raucous, steam rises from the wet pool deck. In the shallow end a little boy stares up at her. His arms, encased in blown-up rings, float on the water's surface. The father looks to see what's caught the boy's attention.

What do they see, she wonders. What does anyone see. Not what they used to. James was the last.

She is every cliché in every book. She will confess to Thomas.

* * *

What do you think will happen if you confess?

I will lose Thomas and the children. All that history, wiped out.

Do you feel you have Thomas?

A version of him. The version that doesn't know what I've done. The version that doesn't know I think about getting on a plane to California every day.

You could say the same thing about losing Thomas, even if you stay. Eventually, everything you know—home, family, church, livelihood, your own body—will betray you. Death of loved ones, abandonment of children, grandchildren; the gradual apathy of friendships, the fall from moral rectitude of clergy and political leaders. Failures of medical professionals. You will be left with nothing but your own mind, and that if you're lucky.

Lucky? My mind is a hell. It replays, on endless loop, a single night in Chicago, then punishes itself for doing so.

The practice of meditation is crucial. Eastern religions understand the importance of training the mind. In your case, you might think of it as being your own minister. You must, in a sense, preach to yourself.

I thought the point of meditation was to empty the mind. To observe thoughts as they pass through the brain as one observes clouds drifting across the sky.

But doesn't emptying imply—indeed, require—the removal, first, of what fills the vessel? It is the articulation of thoughts which in fact renders them observable as separate from the self.

Were I to articulate them it would sound like blasphemy. I would say possibly heretical things about the nature of erotic desire. I might not believe the things I say. I would say them anyhow. To see what I say, in order to know what I think, in order to observe. Maybe even detach.

So say them.

I'm afraid I'll leave a giant ink stain on the history of Christendom if I do.

How do you know unless you try?

Fire Sermon

Brothers and Sisters: a litany, a confession, a proposal.

Where desire began: in third grade, my dark-haired friend Anika with the genius older brother whose parents let him turn his bedroom into a chemistry lab, his tree house into the place he slept at night. We weren't allowed in the tree house, Anika and I, but we went up anyhow, lifted his air mattress to find the magazines that showed us our future selves: how our breasts might someday drape along our ribs, what a man might do to us, or two men, or a woman with the men. So many openings! Anika's fingers quivered when she flipped pages, and something in their shape—nails bitten so short the angry underskin showed—loosened a space behind my navel. I liked the feeling. Like a downhill drop riding in the back-seat. Other days I watched her fingers do other things—move checkers, divvy saltines, dress Barbies—but when I said, *Your hands make my stomach feel shaky,* she dropped the paper she was folding into a flapped pick-a-color fortune-teller and balled up her fingers. *That's weird,* she said. *Don't look at them anymore.* Fifth grade, Karen, greasy blond hair and a legato way of doing things—running, walking, speaking, she even blinked in slow motion. Her breasts were the first in our class to form triangular peaks beneath her T-shirts, until one day the triangles were half-spheres. In the girls' bathroom she lifted her shirt: white, white, and in between, three tiny flowers with colored centers, petal pink, sky blue, mint green. The thrill of finding Easter eggs tucked in a tree root. At a sleepover I asked if I could try on the bra. *Only if you let me try your retainer,* she said. We made the exchange, me imagining her breasts attached to my chest and my saliva in her mouth, though she washed the retainer with soap and hot water before pressing it into her palate. Laura, whom everyone called The Queen, five-foot-eleven at sixteen years old, so shy she would crawl under the covers to change at bedtime, until the night she didn't, she stood beside her bed, me sitting on its twin, already in my nightshirt—rows of plastic horses with lifted forelegs and tiny leather reins our audience—stood there in bra and underwear, looking at me, and unclasped. It was as if she were a time-lapse film of ripening fruit on a branch. How could such a thin body contain that—that *much?* What happened inside me, then, made me dive beneath my comforter. I couldn't breathe. When I came out she was in her robe, sitting on the bed, brushing her hair. *Shall we?* she asked, meaning brush one another's hair, something we'd been doing at sleepovers for years. *Not tonight,* I said, and there would never be another night, I stopped sleeping over that summer, and the following year, when I had a boyfriend and she sent me a letter, handwritten on notebook paper, saying that sometimes she missed me so much she thought about ending her life, I had pulled so far away that I'd forgotten what seeing her—what looking at her—had done to me.

It was an easy transfer, female to male: the boy who sucked blood to the surface of my neck till I told him to stop, and who, when he stopped, I begged to keep going; the boy with acne who told everyone he'd had sex with me when in fact we'd never kissed; the boy who broke up with me because—he said—if I kept dating him I wouldn't be a virgin anymore; the boy with epilepsy who touched my breast through clothing, and who cried when he didn't get into Yale, having felt sure his disability would have given him an edge; the boy who showed me how to kiss his ear, how to suckle the lobe and hold—hold—and let my tongue quiver the skin against the roof of my mouth, how he was teaching me to do something else, though I didn't realize it; and the boy who told me the Bible was a crock, I should ignore everything it and my parents and my church taught me and have sex with him, something I refused to do with any of them until college, when I stopped refusing and did it with Thomas, then married him. One and done. Shut the door on the possibility of another love, or another kind of love.

But what I want to tell you now, Brothers and Sisters— what I realize twenty-five years later: the Indian friend in graduate school, a poet, who came back from a trip to Delhi and told me about her massage, *The masseuse didn't stop short at my breasts—they never do in India—and I let her touch, I couldn't help it, it felt, so, fucking, good.* Men didn't make her feel that way, she was a disappointment to men, didn't know how to orgasm with them; also a disappointment to her family because of her inability to enjoy men, and perhaps I might help her, married as I was? *I think you'd be good for me, you could show me things, how to enjoy myself with a man.* She pulled me into her lap, in her dorm room, reached up inside my shirt and traced her fingers over the cup of my bra; and though earlier that day when we'd been out walking I'd noticed, with a soft pulse in my groin, the heavy side-sway of her breasts beneath her tunic, when she pulled me into her lap and reached inside my shirt, I felt no arousal, only fear. Disgust, even. *We're having an affair,* she told our friends later that night, in a flirtatious tone I'd never heard her use. *No we're not,* I said. She left me alone then. A week later, as I sat beside her in the library, we were friends again. She taught me to write my name in Hindi. She was reading a poem by the sixth Dalai Lama—*It's called* Wings of the . . . Crane, she said, *or it could be* Pelican—and she read a few lines aloud, first in Hindi, then in English, translating slowly: *At the tip of a certain mountain, the moon rises from the east like the sun. When it rises in this way, when what is meant for night comes from morning's—actually,* daytime *is better—from daytime's direction, I remember the face of the one close to my heart.* I watched her hand moving backward across the page, thought of the mind beneath her body and when she looked at me I noticed the way her lips curled up and out, and the dark stains beneath her eyes, and I thought of how her poetry readings were religious incantations, all sound and rhythm, and how she'd cut off her hair because she said men found her beautiful and she couldn't give them what they wanted.

I could kiss you now, I said.

We already had our moment, she said.

More: the documentary filmmaker with the buzz cut and nose ring who, I thought, would be classically beautiful if she allowed her hair to grow; the barista with a tattoo addiction and tongue piercing; the yoga teacher whose assists in half-pigeon involved rubbing my inner thighs and pulling them in opposite directions, as if he could split me in two. And M., my

Aquinas professor, who suggested, after a long run together, that we strip down and swim in a secluded pond. *I've never done that,* I said, and he said, *Done what,* and I said, *Skinny-dipped.* He took off his clothes and went in. I followed. The water was freezing but we didn't mind. He got out and I watched him climb the bank, grab the rope swing, and drop in. We took turns, swinging out farther each time, climb bank, grab rope, jump on, wrap legs, swing out, let go. Before getting dressed, we lay on our backs in a sunny spot on the prickly grass and I told him, without turning my head to look, that he was beautiful. I felt perhaps something of the sort should be said and as the older of us by a year felt perhaps I should be the one to say it. *I think the same about you,* he said.

I prayed forgiveness, after. Prayed my heart and body would tend always and only toward Thomas. Prayed the Psalms: *Cleanse me with hyssop, wash this whitewashed tomb, this painted sepulcher, create in me a clean heart, renew a steadfast spirit.* Prayed the Buddhist prayer: *Liberate me from taints through clinging no more.* Prayed, like Saint Augustine entangled with his outward beauties, for God to pluck me out like a coal from the fire. *Pluckest me out O my God.*

But Brothers, Sisters: What if that's the wrong prayer? What if the right prayer is *Let me burn, only walk beside me in the flames?* Remember the Israelites wandering the Sinai Desert led by a pillar of fire. Remember the three men thrown into the fiery furnace, the fourth who appeared among them, looking like a son of the gods, and how the men emerged unsinged. Remember Moses in the desert, *Take off your sandals,* God speaking from within an unconsuming fire.

Listen: in paintings and mosaics of the transfiguration Jesus stands in the mouth of a blue mandorla. I read this in a book about the color blue. The mandorla, the blue author says, is an almond-shaped image that in pagan times symbolized Venus and the vulva. *I do not know the reason for this blue pussy,* the author writes. *But I do feel its color is right.*

It's the shape that seems right to me. Christ enfolded in a woman's flesh. *To know me you must know this—the pleasure, and the pain, of Incarnation.* The tripartite Godhead contained in almond-shaped vulva—Eros as *necessary* to access the Divine. Yet how are we to learn Eros, or hold on to it in our physical bodies, within the confines of monogamous marriage, in which erotic desire dies off? "We are permitted romantic love with its bounty and half-life of two years," Jack Gilbert writes. And then we begin to yearn for what is forbidden. Other men, other women. This is the hopeless condition into which we are born and the central fact—original sin—upon which our faith is built.

But what if (Brothers, Sisters, bear with me) the institution of marriage was given to us as an intentional breeding ground for illicit desire? What if God, in His Divine wisdom—infinite, unfathomable—ordained marriage not *primarily* for the propagation of the species, nor to ensure the cultural and financial stability of the particular societies in which it flourishes, but to place us into a condition in which erotic desire might thrive?

Hear: without the prohibitions against fornication and infidelity, we would sate and sate and sate again, looking always for the next object in which to find fulfillment, we would gratify our longings until we had nothing left to long for, and the ability to long itself died off.

(Exactly, you might say. Nirvana, you might say.)

Apart from the Law we are all addicts.

Apart from the Law there is no Eros.

But obedient to the Law—faithful inside it—we learn to long *acutely.* And longing, unsatisfied, lifts the gaze. Flesh to spirit, material to immaterial. Forbidden love as tutelage. As if God wants us to feel it, requires it, in order to reach us. *With this much yearning, with this kind of reckless abandon, you are to pursue me. I am the only end for which you were created, your food and drink and satisfaction—the fuel upon which the human machine runs, the home and far-off country you've forgotten.*

I know what you're thinking. Backsliding. Lapsarian. To ask God, in prayer, to be allowed to remain in a state of lust? Conformist, subsumed by the culture! You will talk of the sacrament of marriage, keep the marital bed pure, *for this reason a man shall leave his father and mother and cleave unto his wife, what God has joined together etc. etc. . . . .*

You will say I am condoning sin. Constructing an intellectual scaffolding to justify what should be renounced. But I am only saying what C. S. Lewis said: one can renounce the harmful aspects of a particular love without disparaging the love itself.

I have spent a lifetime renouncing, Brothers and Sisters. You, we, a lifetime of renunciation, and if you would call me aberrant, my words evidence of a diseased mind inhabiting a dying planet, I would say that here are intimations of immortality, here are reminders of the glory whence we came, the unified beings we will again become. A dying planet's reach toward home.

So let me burn.

When she gets back to the room Thomas is sitting on the bed. He's dressed in slacks and a collared shirt, his hair wet and combed. He looks scrubbed, as if ready for church, the flush of sunburn in his cheeks.

Let me talk first, he says when she walks in.

I need to tell you something—

No, I want to get this out. Whatever you two had—I drove you to it.

And now he's on his knees, his arms wrapped around her thighs, his head against her stomach.

Get up, Maggie says. I need to look you in the eyes when I say this.

Thomas stands.

I fell in love with him, Maggie says. James Abbott.

I know, Thomas says. I mean, I suspected.

We cut it off in Chicago. We haven't spoken for over a year.

I figured that too. You were different when you got home.

Why didn't you say anything?

I worried you'd lie. I worried I'd push you away if I asked you about it. I worried you'd leave. In the end I decided to trust you to work it out.

He separated from his wife, before Chicago, Maggie says.

Thomas takes a step backward.

Did he fall in love with you?

I don't know.

Are you still in love with him?

I don't know.

You didn't sleep with him, though, right? he says.

And she is on the cusp of saying it, she is moving the words from the back of her throat—*Yes, I slept with him, I fucked was fucked by made love was made love to and it was the best thing in all my life the very best thing*—but Thomas swipes the air as if clearing away smoke.

Don't answer that. I'm such a fuckup. You've always loved me so well and I've just fucked it up. Here. You never saw the real gift.

He hands her the drawstring bag. At the bottom is a tiny silver bracelet—impossibly thin sterling links with a cut-diamond clasp.

It's beautiful, Maggie says.

I feel ridiculous giving it to you now, Thomas says.

I didn't sleep with him, Maggie says. We never even touched each other.

Thank God, Thomas says, falling backward onto the bed.

You're the better man, she says, sinking to the mattress and sitting beside him.

Thomas puts his hand on the small of her back.

Can you ever forgive me? he asks.

So this is where you're going to land? James a lure toward the eternal?

I must land here. The end of this story depends on it.

You can have any ending you want. You're still in the middle.

No matter which ending I choose, all ends in loss. The only end worth pursuing is God.

What if you're wrong? What if, for all these years, "God" has been just a beautiful, and terrifying, fairy tale? What if theology is, after all, just poetry?

Then think of *Moby Dick*. The Whiteness of the Whale, the Lockean end point of the chapter: color as a secondary quality, created by one's perception and the refraction of light. Strip away the lie of color and the palsied universe lies before us a leper. Transfer this idea to love, to James. Could I see him rightly, there would be only blankness. Light itself would be the only real thing left to pursue.

You forget Ishmael's conclusion: as light is in itself no color, yet physically is comprised of all colors in the spectrum, light is an apt symbol for a godless world, all material things combining to form a dumb blankness. In other words, light is the enlightenment of atheism.

I'm no Ishmael. Whose side are you on anyhow?

I am on no side.

Who are you?

The voice of one behind you, saying, This is the way, walk in it.

But I'm the one who's going to tell you how this ends.

You can't know how the future will play out.

Fine. How I want it to end.

There will be grandchildren. Trips to Europe, an Alaskan cruise with helicopter tours of the shriveled glaciers. Funerals for her parents, both retired and still living in Phoenix, dead within six months of one another, cancer. (*How proud you've always made us,* her mother's last words to her, on the phone.) A move to a cottage on Monteagle Mountain, not far from Nashville, the quiet college where Maggie teaches and from which she will retire.

The cottage will be on a pond with a walking path around its perimeter. It is here they will begin to wait. The giving-away, throwing-away, earmarking for relatives, a gradual winnowing of objects. She will keep no jewelry other than her wedding band and engagement ring. Thomas will keep handwritten cards from Kate and Tommy, a few print photographs they saved and framed. Sometimes, when she's alone, Maggie will turn the frames facedown and practice imagining everyone she loves dead. Maybe it's not so difficult to leave a life behind, she'll think. The life one actually lived, the consummated moments, the ones allowed to bloom across the body, slide into memory and fade into forgetting.

It's the unlived life you end up keeping, Maggie will think. The secret life. *It should have been the family that lasted.* A poem, she can no longer remember whose. *Should have been my sister and my peasant mother. But it was not. They were the affection, not the journey.*

She will read the *New York Times,* still in print. One week she'll see, on the front page of the Arts section, that James has come out with a memoir. Sentimental, the review will say. A blight on an otherwise impeccable body of work.

She will never read the memoir. Maybe she's a part of it, maybe she isn't, either way she couldn't bear it.

James will die the following year. Blood clot. She's seventy-four. They are. She never imagined outliving him. She will buy his *Collected Poems* and put it, unopened, on a shelf. Once upon a time she thought there might be a letter, held in trust, to be sent to her upon his death—some final profession, a parting statement acknowledging the imprint of their shared experience on his life. Months will pass, a year, there will be nothing.

Still, she will find herself thinking—fleetingly—of his torso curling into her back. In the car, driving, she'll be caught off guard by the memory of that moment of acquiescence. Spreading of legs, split-second moan. Something she will never feel again, she is resigned to this now. There it sits in her past: the breach in the harmony of things, single melody split into two, antiphonal. Her life after Chicago became a movement through the middle of two opposing songs, listening for moments of union: as when she was on her back on the chaise in Naples, Thomas's mouth on her thighs, recalling the first time in his dorm room—their pure past (it *was* pure, she will think; what a mess, all that guilt) fusing with the present moment on the chaise, and with the memory of James in the room at the Hyatt, showing her what he could do, simultaneously, with his nose, tongue, and fingers.

She'll dream of him only once. The two of them walking side by side in the dark. She can see nothing, only sense his presence beside her. He's in a hurry, about to give an important reading—a prose poem about a corporate scandal—but there is time enough, before he leaves, for him to pause and pull her against him. She moans, hears herself making the sound she made when he kissed her at the airport in Chicago. The sound of water over rock, the agony of erosion—not the fact of the wearing-away but the time it will take.

Wear me down but do it quickly this time, she will think.

He pulls away, and in the sudden widening of dreams-capes, she sees that all along they have been on a path in the Himalayan foothills. They've arrived at a Tibetan refu-gee camp, monks playing a game like kick-the-can, lifting the hems of their robes, prayer flags flapping above. A place she visited, or maybe only planned to visit, in another lifetime.

I have to go now, James says.

When will I see you again? she asks.

A deliberate silence and narrowing of his eyes that means, Never. She spins away and runs up the trail. Ahead, beside a waterfall, a withered woman beckons, repeating a word in Lepcha: *Daughter.*

Get to her, Maggie will think. If I can just get to her.

Take us to the Hyatt.

At three a.m. we realized how hungry we were. We ordered room service and told them to leave it for us, then took the stairs down to a dark ballroom where earlier I'd glimpsed a concert-sized grand piano. I was wearing his shirt and my pencil skirt. James had on nothing but a robe. He lay beneath the piano while I played the gigue.

God I love that piece, he said.

I stopped playing.

I have a confession, I said. When you told me it was your favorite and I said I knew how to play it—that was a lie. I'd never even heard it. I bought the music and practiced for hours so I could record it for you.

Get down here, he said.

I slipped out of my clothing. Crawled beneath the piano, untied his robe, sat overtop of him and moved. His hands on my hips, my head brushing the piano's ribbed underbelly.

Careful, he said.

How is this possible, I said, pausing; then, how is it *possible,* moving again.

If we could keep this, he said. If we could just walk out of here together and merge our lives with no fallout.

We might turn into the same person, I said.

Darling, he said, pulling my forehead down to his. We already are.

On the way to the airport we drank our coffees without speaking. I finished mine, crumpled the cup, and threw it out the window, then—recklessly—lay across James's lap. Behind my ear his fingers tucked, untucked, and retucked a loose strand of my hair. We told the driver to drop us at different terminals.

You know that Linda Gregg poem, I said, the one where she and her lover say goodbye at the train station?

"Asking for Directions," James said.

That's the one. I'm thinking of how she looks through the dirty window and he's looking up at her—the line about how she would take that look into the future—

That moment is what I will tell of as proof that you loved me permanently?

Yes.

Maggie. I'm only going to ask once.

No. We'd end up loathing each other.

I know.

That's it then.

We'll never tell anyone.

Never.

We won't write or call.

I know.

We pulled up to the terminal, I lifted my backpack, slung my purse over my shoulder. There was nothing more to say. I got my luggage out of the trunk. James came around to the curb.

You getting out here after all? the cabdriver called to James through the window.

I need terminal three, James said. Give me a second.

I feel like I should have something profound to say, I said.

James took off his glasses and reached into his shirt pocket. Patted his pants.

I handed him his handkerchief.

I took it, I said. In the hotel. Proof.

He shoved the handkerchief back into my purse and gripped my upper arms.

I'm going to kiss you now, he said.

In the security line I felt as if something should be done with me. That I should be found out, exposed as the bearer of some evidence: a stashed fragment of bone, a capsule sewn into lining. The agent marked my boarding pass with a highlighter. I unzipped the suede boots and laid them in a bin. Removed my outer garment, unscrolled my scarf, and stepped into the scanner. Bleared, bleary, blearing with exhaustion. A bell ringing somewhere. What day was it? Sunday. God.

God. Who neither slumbers nor sleeps, who looks not as man looks, who sees the guiltiest swervings of the weaving heart: You never loved me as you did last night. As you do now.

What if you woke one day to discover the corpse of Christ had been identified definitively? That an irrefutable, airtight scientific study had been devised to disprove the existence of God, and the study had—beyond any conceivable doubt—proved he did not exist? What would you feel?

Despair.

Can I sing about what's waiting on the far side of fidelity? The wide door-swing, the unfurling sky?

Sometimes I see them walking on the path around the small pond in Monteagle. Their backs are turned, they are holding hands. He is stooped with a full head of hair, blue-white, smooth; she is upright, still lithe, her long steel hair brittle. She refuses to cut it short like other women her age. He is the gentle one, she the fighter. What hurt them through life, after her affair—the volatility, quickness to anger, the startling sharp tugs toward random bodies, full breasts beneath a loose shirt, glimpse of hair above a navel, outline of pectorals; even, during a conversation with a friend, the swell of lips around certain words; how she would get close to the fire and retreat, crucify those sudden onsets of lust for something or someone else, contain, contain, then give what was left to her husband (though many days it was just her, alone on the marital bed, sometimes four, six times in a row)—this passion is now what saves her, and him. She fights against what time is doing to his ability to inhabit the present, rages to hold every day within the framework of past happinesses, to force his memories to enter and transform the moment. *Remember the walks we used to take in the old neighborhood,* the husband will say, *how the children ran ahead of us, remember how we hid plastic toys in the rock wall*—but the wife will refuse the lapse into nostalgia, will take him outside, when he's strong, to hear the tinny sound of rain in the magnolia leaves. On his weak days she'll stand him beside the sink so he can listen to the sounds the cat makes as it laps water from the spigot— her delicate clipped swallows—and the airplane-like hum of the space heater in the mornings, and he will tell her, again, how the kids used to crowd around it, *They called it the Hot Peter* and the slight stickiness on the round wood table where for fifty-three years they've had breakfast and coffee and dinner conversation, where they played Monopoly and blackjack with the children (for money when they were teenagers; the endings in arguments) and where she'd scrubbed away the green globs of melted fruit snacks (science experiment, microwave)—she is fighting to get it all in, not as memory but as something still living. To crystallize each scene from the past into an object they can hold, now, together.

His mind betrays him. He says *teacup* for glass, *dryer* for razor. She cooks with spices she's never used, changes room fresheners. Stasis, she thinks, is the enemy. Stasis is where the end begins. She works out with a trainer. We trick the muscles, the trainer says, never give them the same exercise twice—and this is what she's attempting with her husband's diminishing senses: changing his shampoo, buying new sheets, repainting bathrooms.

She is putting meals before him. She cannot force him to eat.

They are circling the pond, slowing with each lap. She is dragging, he is stumbling. He loses a shoe and looks around with open mouth, his shirtfront a triangle of sweat. She helps him lower himself to the grass beneath a maple, retrieves the loafer, and slides it back onto his stockinged foot.

She sits beside him. They are quiet. From time to time she fans his face, and her own, with her flattened palm.

At the end of all things, when Love comes and asks me what I know, I will point to them, sitting there in the shade. I will say: This man. This woman.

ACKNOWLEDGMENTS

To my editor, Elisabeth Schmitz, and my agent, Anna Stein: Thank you for your faith in my work, and for giving me, always, the space and freedom to take risks. Continued thanks to my Grove Atlantic family: Katie Raissian, Morgan Entrekin, Judy Hottensen, Deb Seager, John Mark Boling, and Gretchen Mergenthaler. For bringing *Fire Sermon* to foreign audiences, and for their editorial insights, thanks to Paul Baggaley and Kish Widyaratna at Picador, Janie Yoon and Sarah MacLachlan at House of Anansi, and Jessica Nash at Atlas Contact. Thank you to The MacDowell Colony for giving me an "emergency" residency, during which I realized—finally—that this book would come first.

I'm deeply grateful to friends who read early drafts and offered invaluable feedback: Samantha Harvey, Roger Hodge, Elliott Holt, Lisa Brennan-Jobs, and John McElwee. For last-minute help with facts and permissions, thanks to Bo Bergman, Tiana Clark, and Tim Liu.

Finally, to my darling husband and children: Thank you for pulling me out of myself, and reminding me what matters.

* * *

The phrase "God, God, tall friend of my childhood" is a variation on a line in John Updike's "Wife-wooing." The phrase "guiltiest swervings of the weaving heart" is a fragment from "The City Limits" by A. R. Ammons. The novel's final line is inspired by "Looking at Them Asleep" by Sharon Olds. I'd also like to acknowledge John Newton, William Faulkner, Virginia Woolf, C. S. Lewis, Simone Weil, Flannery O'Connor, Thomas Merton, Madeleine L'Engle, James Salter, Lydia Davis, Fanny Howe, Li-Young Lee, Maggie Nelson, and Christian Wiman, all of whose language and ideas informed and influenced the writing of this book.